"Blake! Blake!"

In the first instant, in the shock of him against her, she lay still in his arms, and then a knife of terror cut through her and she thrust her elbows at his throat, twisting her body to escape. Her fists came down on his face, hard blows, and, loosening her fingers, she let her nails dig into his flesh.

With one hand he took her two wrists and pinned them at her waist, wrenching her shoulders. Her head bent back, and she could feel him rip her sweater at the neck.

She tore herself free and fell back against the chair, her eyes wide with fear, crouching there, watching him. His large body stood before her, legs apart, arms hanging at his sides, and there was a trickle of blood running down his cheek. He let her wait. Then he came toward her again, lifting her easily, smiling.

Suddenly she was glad. Suddenly she felt free, light, happy. His breathing came heavy and she shut her eyes. A short smile stayed on her lips, and she heard herself whisper, "Blake! Blake!"

In his own intensity Luke did not hear the name she murmured—her father's.

By the same author:
SPRING FIRE

DARK INTRUDER

by

Vin Packer

WILDSIDE PRESS

READERS •

All characters in this book are
fictional and any resemblance to
persons living or dead is purely
coincidental.

DARK INTRUDER

Chapter One

YOU COULD TELL by looking at her.

She had the same tar-black hair, the same pitch-dark eyes, and the same easy, self-important strut.

From the lowliest swipe on up to the top trainer, they all knew her. She hung around the track morning, noon, and night, clocking the geldings, watching the grooms rub down and steam the stallions, and sitting up on the fence near the paddocks, talking pace with the owners.

She mimicked everything about him, from his thundering temper and his fast laughter to his strong, blasting language and his passion for horses, speed, and form.

Jett Black . . . She even had a name like a horse. She was Blake Black's daughter from the word go.

The house they lived in was a small, squarish structure built of gray field stone. There wasn't another house like it in that part of the Shenandoah Valley. It was solid and unique, the outer walls only nine feet high, with tall picture windows eight feet square at frequent intervals, each with a heavy hanging that gave privacy. There was an immaculate green lawn in the front, a wide slate-floored porch in the back, and a full-grown cedar hedge winding around the grounds.

The house sat on a high hill overlooking Bel Air Track and the town of Hillsboro, a small Virginia town filled with farmers and the families of the Daughters of the American Revolution. It was a symbol in Hillsboro, a symbol of the wealth and the defiance of the two people who lived there. Because nobody liked them—nobody but one person, Vince Gellert. Gellert was Black's manager, his right-hand man, and his personal champion, and he liked both of them just fine.

She was standing there on the corner of Foote Street and Jefferson Avenue that morning, waiting for Vince to come along in the pickup. The breeze made the dress cling sharply to her body, outlining the pointing oval breasts, the narrow waist and slight hips, the young, hard thighs, and the long legs with their fine, thin ankles. It was an August morning, sunny and hot, with the smell of honeysuckle and sweet olives in the air, and she was wearing a plum-colored cotton dress with white pearl buttons and white spike-heeled shoes. Her face had a polished-ivory look and her black hair spilled down to her shoulders and was the color of her eyes, which looked straight ahead of her with a you-go-to-hell expression. And that was the way she felt about Hillsboro, its dusty streets, its gaudy bars and cheap fabric stores, and its staring, gawking people.

She felt that way about Dr. Sellers, too. He was a kindly old type, impartial and friendly, with an easy Will Rogers brand of philosophy, and he always wore the same frayed black suit and ragged straw hat. She was standing there when he came up to her.

He said, "Hello there, Jett. Waiting for Vince?"

"He's late," she said. She didn't look at him, but straight ahead, her foot tapping the curb impatiently. There was a brazen quality about the girl, an aggressive, bold contemptuousness wholly divorced from the shy, retiring ways of her mother.

Dr. Sellers could remember Jett's mother, Nan Black, where other people in Hillsboro couldn't, because she'd een a pale, sickly woman, constantly requiring his serv-.ces. Her trips into town had been rare, and for the most part she'd spent her time in that house, dressed in a dusty pink gown and bed jacket, living on pills and sour-tasting liquids and the quick, fleeting smiles Blake Black condescended to give her. Dr. Sellers had brought Jett into the world, and in the same hour he had gone to the room where Blake was waiting and told him his wife was dead. In the moment of silence after he had said those words, Dr. Sellers had witnessed a weird expression of relief and satisfaction in Blake Black's eyes. Then the look changed back to the standard one of impassive coldness, and Blake had thanked the Doctor and told him in that brisk business tone that he would attend to all that was necessary.

That was over eighteen years ago, and the fact that there had ever been a woman named Nan Black, a wife to Blake Black, a mother to this high-spirited girl, seemed ridiculous and mythical. Dr. Sellers shook the memory from his thoughts and concentrated on the girl standing before him. Jett seemed unusually nervous that morning.

"You're all graduated from high school now, eh?" he said.

She said yes and thank God for it. The graduation had come at the end of May, and Blake Black had made one of his infrequent public appearances for the occasion. When she received her diploma she ran back to find him in the audience, and didn't stay on the platform the way the others did. She hugged him and clung to him and

Hillsboro stared and shook their heads and you could tell he was embarrassed. She had on a white net dress that glistened and shone, tight on her figure, and he kept taking her hands down from the shoulders of his well-cut dark suit, straightening his black knit tie, and looking about him red-faced. Abe Herbert, the Hillsboro druggist, was there for his son's graduation, and he sat next to Blake, and he heard him say, "Jett—not here!"

And she said, "Why? I'm so happy! Why?"

And he said, "Because these goddamn rubbernecks are always . . ." and he didn't finish the sentence.

"Well," Dr. Sellers said, "suppose you'll be going to college in the fall."

She said no, she'd be staying right at Bel Aire with Blake, where she belonged.

"You and your dad are thick as thieves," Dr. Sellers said, chuckling, watching her face, which was tense and angry, her eyes bright, but not meeting his. There was something about her that morning, he knew. Something restless, almost afraid.

"I like Bel Aire," she said, for an answer, and then the pickup truck came, with Vince at the wheel, smiling and waving at her.

Vince was a young man, about thirty, with fiery red hair, a stubborn pug nose, and white teeth that perpetually flashed in a broad, easy grin. If he could be called a friend of Jett's, he was the only friend she had. Throughout her years of school in town, she remained aloof and distant with those her own age, as well as those who were older than she. With Vince, she laughed and talked almost as much as she did when she was with Blake. But the closeness was not there physically. She never held on to him the way she did to Blake, and whenever she rode in the pickup she sat far over on her side of the seat. There were no pet names, no long looks, and none of the servile humility.

Perhaps the reason she liked Vince was that it was

next to impossible to dislike him. Impossible even for someone like Jett Black. He had a contagious good humor, a soft, pitiable quality to his baby face, and an earnest, crying interest in you, whoever you were. Hillsboro never wanted to like Vince Gellert because of his connection with Blake, Jett, and Bel Aire, but there was no real defense against his disarming manner, his wide grin, and his eager, wistful greeting. Before long he was a favorite, and the stock answer to his association with the Black world was "Vince is a good sort, and after all, a man's gotta make a livin'."

He was cut above Hillsboro too, an Easterner who had worked as an accountant in New York, and served as a general's aide in World War II, and gone to college, and talked good grammar. By an odd twist of thinking, those things that had been held against Vince Gellert when he had first come to work for Blake were the things Hillsboro pointed to with pride after he won them over. "Bright boy!" they said. "He's all right, Vince is."

He stopped the truck and leaned out to say hello to Doc Sellers, and Jett went around the side and got in. When he cut the motor, Jett nudged him. She said she was in a hurry. Vince winked at Dr. Sellers. "You heard what the lady said." He smiled, turning the key back on and pushing the starter. "I'll be around later tonight. Got a poker game on?"

"You bet," the old man said, and Vince said he'd clean up for sure. Then the pickup rumbled off toward the end of Jefferson Avenue and the turnoff to the long mud road that led toward Bel Aire.

"What's your hurry this morning?" he said.

"You see Blake yet?"

"Saw him about seven-thirty. Up early today."

"What was he like?"

"What do you mean, what was he like?"

"What was he *like*?" she said. "Was he upset or anything?"

"Should he be?"

"Oh, for God's sake!" she said. "Can't you answer a question? Can't you just answer a question?"

Vince looked at her and looked away, back at the road. There was something wrong, something between them, Jett and Blake, that was wrong. He'd acted funny that morning when Vince had told him he'd found a Blue Larkspur to breed. It wasn't easy to come by a mare like that, and Blake was crazy for a high-class colt, and there it was in the making, and Blake had only stared at the papers on his desk and said nothing. Vince had said it over again, not sure he'd heard, and Blake's voice had cracked out like a whip: "O.K., O. K. You got a Larkspur. That's what you're here for, isn't it?"

And now Jett was acting peculiar. She was the one that asked to ride in town with him to shop, and since when did she shop? And now she wanted to get back fast, and wanted to know about him, what he was like that morning.

Vince said, "You and he have an argument or something?"

"Did you ever see us arguing?"

"Nope."

"Then why the hell would we start now?"

"I don't know," Vince said. "I don't know."

Then she said it again. "Well, what was he like?"

"He was busy. He had things to figure out."

She said, "I'll say he did! Oh, God, Vince! God!"

"What's eating you, honey?"

"Nothing."

"Sounds like it," he told her.

"Nothing that's any of your damn business."

"That's right," Vince said. "It isn't." Still, he wondered. It wasn't like them, those two. Rarely, maybe once a year, it was like them to flare up suddenly over something, something to do with the colts, usually, and the way Jett broke them in. It was as quick as it was sudden, and it didn't last this way, or make them brood or snap at other people. Only one time did they get close to the way it was that morning. Vince remembered that time clearly.

It was on a Sunday a year or so back. There were people out at the track, jockeys and trainers, owners and a few people in from town—the usual crowd. It was her birthday, and Blake had promised her a colt, and he'd brought it out to the paddocks that morning. It was a cream-colored mare with a black forelock, mane, and tail, and a black stripe along the middle of her back. It was tall and slender, with the stamina of the wild horse and the speed and grace of the racer. For Jett, it was the perfect one.

She stood there, the white blouse well filled out, tucked in her navy jodhpurs, her boots shiny and polished, and Blake led the colt out to her. The colt looked at her, snorted, reared, flung her head high in the air, and came down beside Jett, tucking her nose affectionately under Jett's arm. And Jett took one hungry look at that colt and then climbed all over Blake, kissing him on the cheek and the neck, crying and telling him thanks and calling him Bunny, the way she did sometimes.

It was the people all around that made him pull away self-consciously. His eyes went from person to person, about half a dozen of them, standing around by the railing. Vince was holding the colt steady and he remembered the way Blake had said, "Easy, Jett! Easy!" and the second easy was loud and irritable.

She had said, "What's the matter with *you?*" but she didn't have to ask. She knew he didn't like them all seeing the two of them like that.

For about three quarters of an hour, she had that dark look and she didn't say much, but after that it was all right and the two of them were laughing and talking about how to train the colt.

Vince could not remember many other times when things had been even slightly strained between Jett and

Blake. They looked alike, they talked alike, they thought alike, and they lived alike—together. Vince envied them because no one could intrude on them, and God knows, if anyone wanted to, it was Vince Gellert. He had started working for Blake when Jett was a kid, fourteen years old, and he had watched her grow. Everything about her grew fast and magnificently, from the wild spark of fire inside her to the beautiful classic features of her face and the mellow ripeness of her body. She was all woman, but for Vince, for anyone who knew her and was not her father, she was like a fine picture of heathen beauty created by a devil artist who had made her precious and unobtainable. Whenever he was close to her that way, Vince wished he could possess her or be possessed by her. But there was Blake, whom he respected and feared, and more than that, there was a passive resignation in Vince's nature that kept him from betraying even his slightest feeling for Jett Black, to her or anyone.

"We're almost there now," Vince said to break the silence.

"He'll be at the track, won't he?"

"I imagine."

"Then I don't want to go to the house. Drive down by the track."

"Jett, if there's anything I can—"

"Oh, Vince, drop it!"

"You just seem nervous, that's all—wringing your hands and getting worked up. I thought—"

"What?"

"That it'd help if you told me."

"It wouldn't," she said. "It wouldn't help a damn thing!"

Chapter Two

It was the morning after graduation, three months back from that morning, when Blake gave it to her. She was in the kitchen, fixing his breakfast, wearing a pair of his old blue-and-white striped pajamas with downy brown slippers on her feet. The sleeves and legs of the pajamas were rolled up to fit her arms and legs, and the shoulders fell off and came halfway down her forearm. Her hair was loose and long, and there was a blue ribbon holding it back. She heard him whistling from the far end of the house where his room was, and she cracked an egg and held it up over the frying pan, letting it plop down into it and sizzle softly.

She called to him then, and waited, facing the door, anticipating the clean, fresh sight of him in the morning. When he came toward her, his thick dark hair was still wet from the shower and his face was smooth-shaven and tanned from his hours of working with the colts in the fields during those late spring days. He had on a pair of neat brown jodhpurs that fitted close, and a rough heavy tweed coat with a crisp white shirt underneath. His black boot heels clicked on the linoleum as he came across the kitchen, holding a hand behind his back.

He said, "A present!"

"Bunny!" She tried to reach behind him to get the package, but he held it higher, laughing. She tugged on his coat and ran around back of him, jumping up to his hand to grab the box from him. When she had it, they were both laughing, and she was tearing at the ribbon on the white paper, ripping it off until she could lift the lid of the box and pull the inside tissue apart. It was a nightgown, a sheer, snow-colored one, sleek and silken, with a look of rich and delicate loveliness, feather-light

13

and soft. Jett took it up in her hands gently, as though it were a living thing, and held it to her breast, her eyes beginning to swim.

"Bunny, Bunny, Bunny, oh, Blake," she said breathlessly, holding it like that. "A gown so beautiful!"

He had been watching her carefully, drinking in the pleasure that came into her eyes, and his own eyes were misty too, but then when she said his name, he laughed and straightened up.

"Maybe you'll stay out of my pajamas now," he said.

"I'm going to save it."

"For when?"

"I'm just going to— It's so beautiful, Bunny! It's—"

She couldn't finish. A tear came from her eye and started down her cheek. Blake moved near her, reaching his hand out, and suddenly in that moment smoke poured up through the room, and the egg in the pan under the open flame turned black, and smelled of burning.

"Hell!" she said. "I forgot your egg, Bunny!"

Riding along with Vince that morning, Jett remembered it well. She had put the gown in a top drawer of her dresser with lilac sachets hidden in its folds, and the tissue underneath to protect it from the wooden surface. It was the only gift like that which Blake had ever given her. There were stirrups and saddles, the colt, the brown hard leather whip, and the hand-sewn boots in past years —impersonal things that she had wanted, and treasured because Blake had bought them for her. The gift of the gown was unique, a turning point, perhaps, she had thought, to show that she was no longer Blake's horse-crazy brat, but a grown lady with a woman's needs.

It was shortly after that that she had first thought a great deal about her dead mother, wondering what she had been like, and she and Blake together. There were no pictures, and there was no mention of her from Blake's lips, and growing up without those things, Jett had never been curious enough to ask him about her in any detail. And then she did, one evening in July, when they were across the dinner table from each other, in the candlelight he loved so well.

"Did she like it too, Blake? Lighting the candles to eat by?"

"Who?"

"M-mother. You know."

He looked surprised, his eyes darting from his plate to meet Jett's.

"What makes you bring her up?"

"I don't know. I wondered, I guess."

"She didn't light candles at the table," he said. "She rarely ate anyplace other than in her own room, on a tray."

"Then she was never really very well?"

"Let's say," he said, "she never thought she was."

"And pretty? Was she pretty, Blake?"

"When she was your age, perhaps. . . . Yes, she was."

Jett leaned forward, her eyes bright and excited. "How pretty? Beautiful?"

"Yes, I suppose she—"

"As beautiful as I am, Blake?"

He put his napkin from his lap to the table and looked at Jett. His voice was low, barely audible, but she had heard him say it. He said, "No!" quickly, harshly, and then, pushing back his chair, and rising as though he had never said it at all, he said, "You *are* a vain little creature, Cricket," and smiling, "Now, how about some coffee? You know, I saw you work out Aurora this morning. I think she'll be ready for the fall trotting meet."

They had never spoken of Nan Blake after that.

Vince turned the pickup on the mud road, and Jett could see the white fence of the track and the red brick buildings, with the stables and the shacks to the left. She

turned the window knob around so it came down and she
could feel the breeze more on her face. It was a surprisingly cool wind, inconsistent with the hotness of the
day and the sticky, motionless air of the night before.

It had been one of those scorching nights in the summer when you couldn't sleep, but only lie there on the
sheets and move restlessly, feeling the dampness of your
own skin. Jett had been awake for hours, and finally,
getting up naked from the bed, she went to the window,
large and wide, facing the track down there. There was a
moon, big and yellow as any, and it flooded the whole
room with its light as she stood there. Her breasts were
high and firm and her skin had a clear, burnished look,
like that of a marble statue. She turned sideways to see
her reflection in the mirror across the room near the
dresser. Standing there, she loosened the ribbon holding
her hair and tossed her head so that the black locks
fell to her back.

Jett felt a new excitement pulse through her, a wild,
sensual freedom, being there alone like that in the early
morning hours. She walked slowly toward the mirror, the
palms of her hands spread open on her hips, her chin
high, a look of defiance in her dark eyes, as though she
were challenging herself to some secret adventure. Reaching in the top drawer where the gown was, she took it
out and held it to her. Then, raising her arms, she pulled
it up over her. The gown hugged her warm, white body
not too tightly, so that through the thinness of the fabric,
each part of her showed faintly.

Jett moved back from the mirror, and without bothering to put slippers on her bare feet, she opened the door
of her room and went down the hall of the house. There
was a clock near the screen leading to the porch and
the hands met at three. She pushed past the screen and
went out on the veranda, crossing to the chair near the
end of the stone floor, facing toward the fields. Everything—the hedge, the high weeds beyond it, the wooden

post, and the white iron furniture—was bathed in that crystal light, and sitting there, Jett felt a restless sense of pleasure looking at all of it. This was what she knew and loved, this house and the land near, and down the hill, the track. She touched the gown with her hand and loved the downy feel of it, the look of it that this night was made for.

She didn't hear him until he was behind her.

He said, "Couldn't you sleep either?"

She got up and stood facing him. "Hello, Bunny."

Suddenly it was different. He was looking at her in a strange way, as though he had never seen her before. She wanted to think of something to say. Blake was there and she was not able to think of anything to say! She realized that she had never worn the gown before, that he had never seen her this way.

She said, "I just put it on."

When the words came, the sound of them surprised her. They sounded faraway and weak, and his did too. He said, "Hot!" his voice thick and cracked, and he looked away from her toward the hedge.

"Yes, it is. I—couldn't sleep."

He didn't answer. She could hear the silence. "Blake?"

"Yes."

"I— Did you ever know it to be this hot? I couldn't even—" She went closer to him, her hand touching his shirt sleeve. "Blake?" His arm pulled away in a jerk. "What's wrong, Blake?"

He looked at her, a long look at the whole of her, and then he caught her quick and pulled her to him. His mouth was as hot as the night itself, and it fed on her lips, his fingers digging into her arms. Her body shook and throbbed, and her hands grasped his hair and held to it, an exquisite pain thrilling her nerves, stifling the high cry that caught in her throat.

A minute, an eternity—and finally the hand slammed hard against her cheek, pushing her down on the floor.

She heard him scream out, "Oh, my God! My God!" and lying there with the gown torn clear of her shoulders, she saw him turn and stride off toward the hedge and the night, her own heavy sobs following him.

When she woke up that morning, she had slept for a bare half hour, a sleep of exhaustion and semiconscious dreams, the sheets on the bed rumpled from the persistent twisting and turning. She dressed quickly, running from room to room, fear mounting inside her each time she found a room empty.

He was gone, and she knew he was gone, even when she shouted his name and banged the doors shut. Running down the hill toward the track, and past the negro shacks and the smell of bacon cooking for breakfast, she came to the gate and the paddocks and the red-brick building where his office was. And she saw him, standing there, talking to a groom. She stopped and looked at him, realizing that there was nothing she could do—certainly not go to him; not then and maybe not ever go to him, because she knew Blake. She knew that he was cut through and bleeding with what had happened, sick and humiliated and sorry, and she knew too that she was not. That was not the reason she had cried last night.

"Well, honey," Vince said, pulling up to the gate and turning the motor off, "I'm glad you came along."

She got out and closed the door. Behind the barn near the gate she could hear the Negroes playing craps, calling out numbers and giggling. She walked on the gravel path leading toward the brick buildings, hearing the steady crunch as she came closer.

"Whatever it is," she heard Vince call out, "I hope it works out O.K."

Chapter Three

It was his own fault. Blake drew a row of squares at the bottom of the list he had been preparing, squares and circles and straight lines, and he reached to his left, where the steaming hot coffee was cooling in the cup. He put it to his lips, scorching them slightly, and then he banged the cup back in the saucer and swore.

He had told Nan that he did not want a child. He *never* wanted a child. Nan had planned it despite his wishes, to prove something—perhaps to prove that she was not sickly, not really, not the way he had accused her of being during the many years of their marriage. Remembering those years, Blake flinched at the thought of the scenes, ugly, sordid scenes between Nan and himself.

"Blake, I'm not ill. I'm just—well, more delicate than most women. I'm—fragile." And he would ask her to get up, please for the love of God not to stay in that bed day after day, that it would make anyone weak. That was before he had the track, shortly after their marriage.

Those early years after they had bought Bel Aire and built the house, Blake had encouraged her to see Sellers, the Hillsboro doctor, and Sellers had left bottle after bottle of multicolored pills and thick liquids, attempting to "build her up," but her sickness was in her mind, rooted there like a tree's roots. Blake had suggested a trip to a psychiatrist in Richmond, and the insinuation that her mind needed a doctor's care drove Nan to a frenzy unequaled in their years together.

"We'll have a baby," she announced casually one evening when he brought her tray to her room. "Then you won't be so preoccupied with all this animal, physical business that I hate."

"That isn't the answer, Nan."

19

But Nan had thought it was, and Jett had been conceived. He had never wanted her, but as she grew, a love grew in him that was stronger and greater than any he had ever known. It was impossible for him to believe that she had sprung from Nan's womb, and equally impossible for him to believe that she was his daughter, and he her father.

His fist became a knotted ball of flesh, and he brought it down hard on the wooden desk top, closing his eyes, his mind crawling with vivid pictures of the night and the moon and the way Jett had looked in the gown and what had happened there. Inevitable? He wondered if it had been, or if with more careful awareness he could have avoided that moment. But how do you know, he thought, how do you know such an emotion is growing, extending off and becoming something divorced from its beginning, something abnormal and fearful? Incest! He wanted to hang himself, or her, or both of them. Shaking his head like a dazed man who had been clubbed and kicked hard, he picked the pencil up and tried to begin again with the list. It made him sick —the idiotic names written there, the numbers after each one, the whole asinine plan made him sick. But what else? What else was there for him to do?

"Busy?" Jett shut the door behind her and came to stand beside him. Her voice was tight and restrained, and he did not look up at her, but stared straight ahead at the paper before him.

"Just working over some things," he managed.

"It's almost lunchtime."

"I know."

"Would you like a ham sandwich? We have some ham left from—"

"I think I'll eat here today, Jett. Get some eggs from the shack or something. Quicker."

"Then you aren't coming up to the house?"

"No."

"Blake, I—" She did not finish the sentence, and for a few fixed seconds there was a tense stillness, relieved by the scraping noise Blake's chair made as he pushed it back and got up to walk to the window. His back was to her, the dense sable hair above his white collar, the long, husky shoulders, the tall figure, his hands shoved into the pockets of his jodhpurs, his dark green tweed coat flapping out in back.

He said, "Jett, I've made out a list of colleges."

"For who?"

"I thought you could go over them and decide which one you'd like to attend."

"I can tell you now," she said. "None of them. I don't want to go away."

His words droned on, his eyes looking straight ahead of him, through the windows out to the pastures where the colts were romping. "You'll have to do it quickly. It's late for registration and I think—"

"I don't want to," she cut in. "I don't want to go to *any* college."

"It isn't a case, Jett, of what you want to do." The tone in his voice was steady, even. "Or of what I want to do."

"I'm not going to any hellhole of a college, Blake!"

He turned sharply, staring hard at her, almost shouting that the list was on the desk, that she should pick a college from the list on the desk.

"Because of last night," she said, above his shout. "Because of that I have to go to college! So that's the way you're going to handle it! Don't talk about it! Pretend it never happened! Just pack Jett off to some institution!"

"I don't want you to mention last night, *ever!* Do you understand?" He stood there, his legs apart, his hands clenched at his side.

Jett looked at him, her face filled with wrath. "I understand fine! Get rid of me and then you've got no problem. Well, you *have* got a problem. My going isn't going to help, Blake, it isn't! You don't know what you're doing!"

She leaned on the desk, her head bent, her coal-colored hair falling down at the sides of her face, and her voice had a vibrant quiver that made the tone go higher as she spoke. "I suppose college is going to help me. I suppose at some college I'll learn that what happened is abnormal! God, Blake, don't you think I know what it is with us? What's college going to teach me? Not a damn thing! But I'll be out of your way, won't I? You'll be here, here where everything I love is, and me, I'll be in some classroom learning nothing! Nothing because I don't want to learn what they teach there! I want to be here, Blake!"

"No!" Blake moved back from her and sank into the chair near his desk.

"Blame it on me, now. I've got to get out because it was my fault. Well, it wasn't, it wasn't! Who bought me the gown, Blake? Remember, you bought me the gown. You grabbed me, Blake! Oh, God, Bunny, Bunny, why? Why did you let it happen, Bunny?"

Blake brought his hands up to his face to cover his eyes, his shoulders shaking, his lips saying her name and saying, "Don't! Don't! Don't!" until the words stuck in his throat and emerged in a gruff, halting half sob.

She stopped and stared at him then, not believing what she saw, crossing over to him to touch his sleeve.

"Bunny, I'm—I'm sorry." He could not look up. His hands trembled before his face, and there were slight moist tears running down his long fingers. Jett sank to her knees beside him, her hands clutching at his boots. She said, "Bunny. Bunny," and then, "Blake! Oh, Blake!" and her own sudden sobbing kept her from saying more.

Chapter Four

"H e's a solid, blocky chestnut with good bones," Dud Thomas said, helping himself to the corn bread. "A bit short in the leg, but his pasterns is the right length."

Vince wiped his mouth with the oversized paper napkin and grunted an answer. It was always as hot as a furnace room in the mess shed that time of year, and Vince barely managed to get his food down before the heat beat him and he had to shove his chair back and push his way past the flies, out the door to the air. That noon, Blake met him halfway, standing at the doorway with the screen pushed open until one of the handlers, not knowing it was Blake, yelled out, "Fer the love of Mike, shut that door—we're eating flies as it is!"

It was a surprise to see Blake there. The nearest he ever came to the mess was when he sometimes walked along at the end of Shed Row to find one of the rubbers to give hell to for something. Then he never did come inside the mess, but sent a boy down to the shack if he was hungry, and took the stuff back to his office and ate it there.

Vince thought it was probably about the Larkspur, and he let the door bang behind them. Out in the sun with the breeze, he said, "Did you see her?"

Blake said, "See who?"

"The Larkspur."

"No."

Vince walked along with him, knowing enough not to press the point, not the way Blake was then. There was plenty in the wind and Vince knew it, but he decided to say nothing.

Blake said, "I'm taking the pickup this afternoon."

Still Vince didn't talk, didn't say how come, and he

knew too that this was something Blake didn't do ever on workdays—take the pickup.

"There's a fellow coming about that cull we're stuck with," Blake said. "See if you can unload the thing on him."

They stopped by the paddocks and one of the grooms was riding Big Chance, a mean horse with too much buck in him. Vince watched Blake look at the groom letting the horse out like that, and he knew for sure then. Because Blake just looked and there was no expression in his dark eyes. Any other day they would have been flashing and he would have been holding on to the rail and shouting at the groom. He would have been shouting, "Hold him in your lap! Hold him in your lap, you damn fool!"

"Well," Vince said after they turned their backs on it, "here are the keys."

Blake took them and Vince stood there while he walked off toward the front where the pickup was parked. Vince started to call out and ask him how long he'd be gone, but then he shut his mouth again. Blake wouldn't have told him, anyway.

Late that afternoon, when Vince was saying good-by to the man who bought the cull, he saw Jett through the window, coming down the walk slowly. She was trying to see in, to see where Blake was, and Vince could see her standing on tiptoe, peering at them from the walk.

"It's a fine horse you bought," Vince said to the man, opening the door, and the man didn't know a thing about horses because he said he thought it was fine too, and he was smiling with pleasure when he tipped his hat and went out, passing Jett on the walk. Vince stood in the doorway waiting for her to come nearer.

"He isn't back yet," he told her.

"Back from where?"

"From wherever he went."

"Great!" she said. "I see you're as clear as ever."

"Didn't you know he'd gone?"

"I don't know anything any more. I don't know. I was with him right after I got back from town with you. Then I went up to the house to fix lunch and—"

"He eat up there?"

"No," she said. "I thought he got something from the shack. I thought he might come up, and I waited, but he didn't."

"He took the pickup," Vince said.

"What would he do in the pickup? Where would he go?"

"Don't ask me," Vince said, squinting, with the sun in his eyes. It was setting off in the sky, a dark red color, and Vince looked at his watch. Blake had been gone close to five hours.

"He didn't take his own car?"

"I said he took the pickup."

"Into town, maybe. But what's in town?"

"You're asking me questions I don't know the answer to."

Jett frowned and shook her head fast, as if she were trying to wake up after a long sleep.

"I got some coffee inside," Vince said. "Want some?"

She followed him into Blake's office, and there was the smell of the steaming coffee on the hot plate. Vince said, "That guy bought the cull. I think I got him doped on so much coffee," but Jett was standing by the window staring out toward the road.

"He'll be back," he told her.

"Vince, where does he keep his keys?"

"I don't know. What the— You can't drive."

"You can, Vince."

"Not *his* car, I can't. Not on your life!"

"We could find him and—"

"Find him where? I don't want to find him. Leave him be. He'll be back."

"He'd be mad, anyway."

"Darned right!"

Vince poured the coffee into two plastic cups and handed her one. She had changed from the summer dress: she was wearing a pair of knee-length shorts that showed her bare legs well, and there was only a pair of moccasins on her small feet. The cotton sweater she wore was thin over her brassiere, and her breasts were full and proud. The black hair was tied back behind her head with a ribbon just as black, so that it could hardly be seen there in the softness of the waves. Vince forced his eyes to look away from her as she sat there staring out at the road.

"You and he have a fight?" he said.

"Maybe."

"He'll get over it."

"How do *you* know?" she answered, but she didn't yell. She just talked quietly, as if she were afraid.

She was thinking that she would not go. Blake could not scare her into going to college like this. Wherever he went, she thought, he will have to come back, and whatever he says when he comes back, it will not make any difference. Even the memory of his sobbing then when she had been with him did not spoil this decision. There was nothing, she knew, nothing that he could do to make her go away from him. Because she knew too that he did not really want it that way. It was only because he was afraid.

Jett was not afraid. Not of that. Of where he was, a little, but not of before he went, and not of when he should come back. There was no shame in her for what had happened, only for the shame that was in him, and she would fight that somehow. Finishing her coffee, she felt stronger for thinking about it.

"Want to ride?" she said to Vince.

"I better wait here. Can't tell what might come up with no one around."

"I'll take Don't," she said. "If Blake comes, tell him I'm out riding Don't."

She had named him Don't because when he was a colt and she was breaking him in by herself, Blake stood at the paddocks yelling, "Don't" at everything she did to the young colt.

"Stop by and see the Larkspur I got," he called after her, but she too was in that other world Blake had been. It was the way she spent her nervous energy, riding like that, and there was none faster than Don't at Bel Aire.

He walked through the hall outside of the office and down to the end of the building, where he could see the paddocks and the fence to the trail. In a while he saw her come out. A boy opened the fence, and she was letting the horse canter easily. But outside the fence, he saw her raise the crop in the air, and then he could only hear the wild beat of hoofs over hard-packed clay, and see the dust and the colored boy standing there waving it out of his eyes.

Chapter Five

I T WAS Willie Kane doing the talking. Big Willie Kane standing there against the white walls of the reception room in Hillsboro General Hospital, holding his greasy checkered cap loosely in his thick hands, fumbling nervously with the black buttons on his heavy plaid wool work shirt, his long square legs hanging out of his dusty work pants, grimy white cord strings for laces in his eaten-out leather shoes. Willie was whimpering as he talked, his fat jowls wiggling nervously, and the way his head hunched over on the right side and hugged his shoulder made his voice sound as though it were coming from inside a tunnel a few yards away. There were four or five people in the room where he was talking, but they knew how the accident had happened and they were not listening to him, and it was as if he were alone in that tunnel talking crazily to himself.

He kept saying, "I was makin' a U down there by the Pike in'ersecshun. I never seen him. Lord, he was comin' like hell on wheels. Lord! I shouldn't of made that U, but plenty made 'em on me and I never rammed 'em. I let 'em know I was coming. Lord, but he didn't. He just came."

Willie kept seeing it, the way he swung the great fruit truck he drove until it made the U turn, and suddenly the darting image of the smaller truck and the slow second before the inevitable collision when he saw Blake Black's face wince hard and wrinkle in horror. The heaviness of the crash had sent Willie forward, his belly lurching into the wheel, his arm clearing through the hard glass in the front window, and his forehead punctured by the black choke knob on the steering board. He could remember the way it felt, and afterward, in the immedi-

28

ate silence, the low moaning of Black's voice for a few
long minutes before it stopped and there was left only
dust and stillness and the sun went too, right then, off in
the sky, leaving only a purple red look where it had been.

Jed Farmer, the cop, had come soon after, but not before Willie had pushed himself out of the seat, kicking
the bent tin door with his foot, blowing the road dust
from his face, and jumping down to the road, limping on
his foot and holding his arm where the warm blood came
through the wool of his sleeve.

Willie stood there then, the pickup a few feet from
him, crushed and twisted, and walking toward it, he could
see the side window broken and the glass with its jagged
points, and he could see the slumped body of Blake Black,
but not his face. Black's head was thrust forward and the
windshield at the front was cracked but not broken where
his chin hit.

It was funny, Willie remembered, what he had done
then. He had stood there looking at the wreck, not going
closer, and his voice had come like a whisper, pleading,
"You all right, Mr. Black? Mr. Black?"

Because he was afraid—not of the wreck, but what if
he was not all right and was dead.

And then he'd done another funny thing, Willie
remembered. He had reached down and picked up a
pebble and he had tossed it so it hit the side of the door
of the pickup, as if he were scaring a bird up from the
bushes, but there was no sound after the pebble rang
against the fender, and no movement from inside.

It was at that moment, after the pebble hit and the
silence came back, that Willie ran, hobbled, went fast to
get away from there. Not to go for help, as he told the
cop, Jed Farmer, when he met him there on the road,
but because he had to go, as if it were a dream he was
running from and when he got out of sight it wouldn't
be there. He did not want it to be there, either, because
that had been his job, driving that truck of fruit, and it

was over now, he knew, whether Blake Black lived or died, it was over and he was Crazy Willie again, running with his head screwed onto his shoulder and twisted.

Farmer said, "What happened, Willie?"

"I was makin a U. He came like hell at me. I didn't see him and—"

"Not supposed to make a U."

"They all do. This road ain't crowded."

"It's against the law, Willie."

"I know, but—"

"Where were you heading for?"

"To git help."

"You'll need it, Willie. Now, wouldn't you know you'd go and hit Black? Out of all the people you could have hit, you picked him."

"He hit me."

"No matter," Farmer said. "Come on, Willie."

Willie never had a good job like that. Driving, with the smell of the oranges and grapefruit and apples and the light green grapes and all coming from the back, and the big truck rolling over the clay roads and around down the hills. He had been an errand boy before, the big crazy boy, there's one in every town, and then he got that job and he was careful too, but it was over now. If Blake was dead, Willie knew, there was more than an end to the driving and the smell of fruit and the way it was, there was more than that to feel bad about.

It was while Willie was standing there in the hospital talking and thinking like that alone that the door opened, and he didn't have to turn to see who it was. Doc Sellers went forward to meet her.

She was wearing the knee-length shorts with the flat moccasins on her feet, and over her shoulder she had a long green suede coat. Her black hair was uncombed and wild-looking, and there was a wet redness to her face, but her eyes were sharp and bright. Behind her, Vince stood uncertainly, a haggard expression on his face.

"He's not conscious yet," Doc Sellers said. "You'll have to wait, and it may be quite a while."

"Is he going to be all right?" Her own voice was strangely quiet too.

"Jett, I think he's got a good chance. I didn't perform the operation—Dr. Kingsley did that, but he's competent and thorough. Everything's being done, Jett."

"Where is he hurt most?"

"His spinal cord. I don't know yet how serious it is. We'll know more tomorrow and the next day. Now, Jett, if I were you I'd go along back to Bel Aire with Vince and we'll keep in touch. No sense being here waiting. Even when he is conscious, I don't think you should see him."

"I've got to be here," she said. "I've got to wait."

She sat down in the green wicker chair near the window, staring out at the darkness. Vince followed her, standing there by her and not saying anything.

Willie was watching her from where he stood, afraid she would look at him and know it was he who had done it. He stood frozen, wanting not to breathe or move, but not able to take his eyes from her. It was different the way she was, like a child, he thought, and not like the fiery girl who strutted through the downtown streets and once had given him a rap on the back with her whip when he was sitting on the curb in the sun and laughed at his startled expression.

She was quiet and he thought yes, she was afraid, and the thought made his blood hot for a reason he could not tell. Her lips were moist and there was a sick, sad look in her eyes, and Willie could see her breasts outlined under the cotton sweater, like the shape of pears he had held often in his large hands and squeezed until they were crushed and he was sorry that he had ruined them that way.

He saw Vince touch the girl's shoulder with his hand and say something soft, and Willie wanted to punch Vince in the jaw and send him rocking backward.

Tim Herriman, a reporter from the Hillsboro Advertiser, broke away from a small group gathered at the end of the room and walked over to Jett.

"Hello, Miss Black," he said, holding his hand out to her. She ignored the hand and barely nodded.

"I was wondering if I could get a picture."

"No."

"This is a big story, Miss Black. People around here heard about you and Mr. Black, even if they've never seen you, and—"

Jett muttered something under her breath and Vince stood in front of her.

He said, "Tim, lay off now, huh? Don't play big-city reporter just now."

"How about one of you, then? One of you and Willie. Talking it over."

"Willie who?"

"Willie Kane."

"Tim, you gone crazy?"

Willie heard his name and he held his cap to his mouth and his teeth bit into the greasy cloth. They did not know yet that he had been the driver of that fruit truck. He looked at the door and he wanted to run, but his feet were bricks and he could not lift them from that spot in the floor.

Tim was telling them and Willie watched Vince's face as a look of incredulous disbelief came on it, and Jett was staring up at Willie, a long look from his dirty shoes to his eyes and his forehead and his wild hair. She slumped back in the wicker chair, her face in her hands.

Willie loped across the room until he came to her. He stood before her. His voice was hoarse and throaty. "I didn't mean to do it."

Her hands still hid her eyes, the full mouth, the beautiful look of her face. Willie felt his knees shake as he watched her.

"I didn't mean to," he said. "I didn't mean to."

The light from the flash bulb spotlighted the scene, and Herriman ran with his camera, colliding at the door with Doc Sellers.

"Leave her alone," Vince said to Willie, and Willie backed away, his eyes fixed on her.

The doctor walked over to Jett and she took her hands down from her face.

"Is he— Can I see him?"

"I think you'd better wait at home for him, Jett. It may take longer than we think."

"Can you tell—anything?" Her voice was so weak that Willie could barely hear it, but he saw her face fully now, the sick worry lines all over her forehead and around her pretty mouth. It made Willie feel strange, as though he had hurt her and not Blake Black, and he did not mind this thought.

Vince took her arm and helped her to her feet. "We'll stay by the phone, Jett. We'll know right away when you can see Blake."

"That's right," Dr. Sellers said. He followed the pair to the door and took Jett's hand. "Don't worry," he said, "and try to get some sleep."

When they were gone, he looked at Willie.

"You better go too."

"He ain't going to die?"

"No, I think he's going to live. Somehow."

"She hates me. You shoulda seen her look at me."

"She's excited, Willie."

"Me too," Willie said, wadding his cap up in his hands. "I'm excited too."

Dr. Sellers told him to take care of his arm and watched him go through the swinging door. He felt sorry for Willie Kane and sure that it had not been Willie's fault. Dr. Kingsley's report of Blake's condition prior to the operation was a unique one, and one that would set many tongues wagging. For as long as Hillsboro had known

Blake, and as long as Doc Sellers himself had known him,
Blake had never taken more than three drinks at one
time, and seldom that. Yet the report had stated clearly
that Blake Black had been thoroughly intoxicated at the
time of the wreck.

There was a cool breeze from the hall as the door
opened. Kingsley had changed from his white uniform
to his brown tweed suit, and his overcoat was on his arm,
the black bag in his hand.

"Well," he said to Sellers, "it's just as we thought."

"It's a miracle, Fred."

"He'll think it's a curse. He'd rather be dead."

"It's still a miracle with a spinal injury like that."

Kingsley took a pipe from his pocket and blew into the
stem. "You going to break the news to her?"

"I guess I'll have to. I brought her into the world, you
know—was her doctor all her young life. I swear, though,
I don't have a minute understanding of the girl. She's an
odd one, and it's going to be a task."

"You want to tell *him* too? When he's stronger?"

"God almighty!" Sellers sighed. "How does a man tell
a man like Blake Black that he's permanently paralyzed
from the waist down?"

"It's a hell of a thing to tell *any* man," Kingsley said,
poking the tobacco into the bowl of the pipe. He struck
a match and sucked in until the smoke started. "See you
tomorrow," he called after him as he went. "Night, Doc."

Blake was weak for eleven days—days during which Jett
plagued Dr. Sellers to be permitted to see her father. It
was not until the twelfth morning that he consented to
this, and not until he told Blake about his paralysis. He
lay awake beyond dawn thinking of a way to say it, but
when he faced Blake at ten that same morning, he said it
bluntly, almost harshly, his words sounding hollow and
strangely ominous in the small hospital room where Blake
lay on his back in the bed staring up at the ceiling.

When he was finished, Blake said nothing at first. His face, pale from the operation and the strain, was blank, but there was a sharp tightness to his jaw, and when he did speak, his tone was dry and cold.

"Permanent?" he said.

"I'm afraid so."

"I don't believe it."

"I'm sorry, Blake."

"I'll see other doctors. I think I believe more in medical progress and genius than you do yourself, Sellers."

"If there were any way, Blake, any way at all, you know I'd—"

"There *is* a way. When I regain my strength, I'll find that way. You and Kingsley have done your duty, I thank you for that. I'll carry on from here."

"I wish I could impress on you that it isn't a case of finding a way, or of finding other doctors. Blake, your paralysis is permanent. The sooner you adjust yourself to that idea, the better you'll be, mentally, physically, and spiritually too."

Blake was impervious to the meaning of Seller's words. The early September sun flooded the room, casting its light on his face, forcing him to shield his eyes with his bandaged hand until Sellers rose and pulled the blinds. When there was less light, Blake raised himself slightly on the pillow, his forehead creased in a thoughtful frown, his fingers snapping nervously.

"It'll mean getting a temporary manager," he said, "someone who knows horses well. I'll be able to supervise from a—a wheel chair." The last words sounded ugly. "Jett will have to help, too. Yes, she'll have to help a lot around Bel Aire now. I'll have to see her, Doctor, immediately. The foals will have to be weaned in—"

Dr. Sellers interrupted him. "She's outside. I'll get her for you. She's been half crazy all week."

He went to the door, and then halted and looked at Blake.

"I've never known you to get drunk, Blake," he said.

"I never had a reason, Doc. And now it looks like I won't have one again for a long time."

"You licked whatever was bothering you?"

Blake laughed for the first time. "Yes," he said, "it was licked in fine style. Funny," he said sourly, "how things have a way of working out."

Sellers said, "Jett will be anxious. I'll get her. By the way, she doesn't know this yet. I didn't know whether I ought to tell her, or whether you wanted to."

"I'll tell her," Blake answered. The smile left his face and the hard line came back to his jaw. There were only slivers of sun entering through the thin slats in the Venetian blinds, and they fell in narrow bars across the floor of the room, and the dust danced inside the narrow strips. Blake shut his eyes and waited for her.

She did not wince or grimace or show any expression on her face, and her first words sent his love for her singing through him.

"I don't believe it's permanent," she said.

"Nor I."

She stood before him then, her eyes fixed on his, and there seemed to be a mutual agreement between them, a pact against any kind of fate that might befall either one of them or both of them together. He held his hand out to her and she reached for it, touching the bandage first and then sliding her fingers down to his fingers and feeling the warm flesh and the hardness of his knuckles. She sat at the edge of the bed and her arms went to his shoulders.

"I was afraid, Bunny," she told him. "I was so terribly afraid."

He said, "It's all right now," and there was a determined sound to the words when he repeated them. "It's *all right* now, Cricket."

Chapter Six

"What's he like?" Jett asked. She handed Vince the tweed jacket from the hall closet. "I think Blake'll need this today. Cooler out, isn't it?"

Vince took the jacket and put it over his arm. He leaned against the wall in the doorway to the kitchen as he talked to her. She was still wearing her robe, a heavy wool one in a deep green color. On the table behind her Blake's tray was clean of food, and only the soiled dishes were left, and a single crust of toast.

"He's a damn fine horseman, for one thing."

"How do you know? He hasn't even been here a day."

"His record. He's got a hell of a record. You know, he was Blue Streak's trainer. And before that, he ran Hill Valley. Don't kid yourself, he's a good man."

Jett smiled. "As good as Blake?"

"You're prepared to hate him, huh?"

"No," Jett answered, "just to resent him a little. Him or anyone!"

"Well, *he* didn't do it to Blake. Anyway, according to Blake, he's just temporary."

"Do you believe it, Vince?"

Vince looked at her and suddenly he wanted to shout at her—to tell her no, he didn't believe it, that it was a flimsy, futile dream that she and Blake were indulging in, that Blake was paralyzed and that was the cold fact, and that was the way it was. Instead, he moved away from the wall, shifted the jacket to the other arm, and said, "I don't know, Jett. . . . Better take this to him now."

"But you didn't answer my question."

"I said I didn't know."

"I mean my question about Mr. Hetherington. What's he like?"

"I only know what he's like with horses. You'll have to meet him yourself."

"I intend to," Jett said, "later."

Vince turned and walked down the hall to Blake's room. He wondered if Blake really believed that his paralysis was temporary, or if it was a role he made himself play for Jett. Because it had been Blake who had studied Hetherington's record so carefully, and it had been Blake, and Blake alone, who had insisted on Hetherington for the job. Only a fool would hire Luke Hetherington for a temporary position. A fool, or an impetuous, arrogant egotist.

Blake was sitting in the wheel chair looking out the window when Vince came into the room.

"Here's the coat," he said. "All set now?"

"I'd like my boots."

"But Sellers said you should try the slippers for a few months."

"The boots are in the closet. On the floor."

It was not so easy to be a nurse to Blake. Jett was better equipped to ignore the Doctor's orders and to answer Blake's needs unquestioningly, and it was she who did the bulk of this work. Vince had a small part, dressing Blake in the morning and helping him in the evening, and gradually he was learning not to interfere with Blake's impulsive demands despite their inexpediency. He knew too, that this part of Blake's misfortune *was* temporary, because every day Blake was learning to do more and more unassisted. Eventually, Blake would dress himself and everyone would be satisfied. Jett would no longer resent Vince's intrusions, and Vince would be able to concentrate all of his energies on the track, as he had done before. He would not have to see Jett in the early morning when she looked sleepy and beautiful, and in the evening he would not have to feel the gnawing ache after he left the house and walked down the hill to the bunkhouse alone.

The boots fitted tight over Blake's legs, and Vince had to struggle hard to pull them on. When it was done, Blake said, "All right now, let's go meet this miracle man Hetherington."

"He might not be at the office yet."

"Why the hell not?"

"I think he's swimming."

"Swimming!"

"Yeah," Vince said. "I saw him earlier going toward the quarry. Said he wanted to cool off."

"I thought you said it was cooler out."

"Plenty cool out," Vince told Blake, pushing the chair through the door. "Maybe he's warm-blooded."

Luke Hetherington stretched.

He was standing at the edge of the cliff. The water below him was a thin blue ring that circled around the jagged rocks and went deep into the belly of the earth. A swift breeze nudged the brush and the tree branches near where he was standing, and a cloud traveled over the yellow sun and cut off the brightness of the light momentarily.

His body leaned back against the sky. It was a body of long straight lines, hard and firm and tall. He stood rigid, his shoulder blades drawn tight together, the curve of his neck rigid too, and his hands, hanging at his sides with the palms spread out. In the hollow of his spine he felt the cold air blowing against him, up his back, tossing his hair playfully. His hair was neither white nor blond, but the exact color of sea sand swept ashore and parched in the sun. His high cheekbones accentuated the hollow cheeks, and the straight even nose above the tight mouth with its large tight lips. His eyes were blue as the water below, but steady and cold.

He stepped to the edge of the cliff, raised his arms, and dived down into the ring, hitting the water with a splash and a great spray. Then, cutting straight across, he reached the rocks where his clothes were, and a small boy sat laughing and waiting for him.

"Through swimming?" he said to the boy.

"You looked like a bird," the boy laughed again, "coming down from the sky. Then you were a fish."

"You look like a landlubber," Luke said, stepping up from the water and shaking his head to clear his ears.

The boy had the body that a boy of six has, with the same blue eyes as his father's, and the same towhead. He watched his father, imitating him, as he saw him pull his old denim trousers on, and pull the white cotton sweater over his wet head. It took the boy longer to tie the strings on his white sneakers, and Luke waited for him until he was finished.

"O.K., Raol?"

"O.K.," the boy said, and the two cut across to the path leading through the woods and back to the track.

Blake was waiting in front of the brick building, his wheel chair facing the opening through which they came. Hetherington was walking slow and easy, looking down at the small boy, talking and grinning at him, as he came up the path and stopped abruptly at Blake's side.

"Mr. Black," he said. "How are you?"

He pushed the boy gently in front of him. "This is Raol, my son."

"I didn't know you were married, Hetherington."

"My wife died," Luke said.

Blake pushed the wheels of his chair as they went along. "I'm sorry if the cabin looks a little shabby. We had to clean it out fast when we knew you were coming immediately."

"It's fine for us."

"I hope the boy won't get bored with no other kids around."

Raol said, "There's Jiffy."

"Who?"

"Jiffy," Raol repeated.

"The cook's kid. Raol met him this morning," Luke explained.

"I forgot about the help," Blake answered. "Well, you seem to be well acquainted with everything."

"I've got the setup," Luke said, "and I think I can manage. I'd like to hire someone for my truck and odd jobs."

Blake looked at him, admiring his confidence, knowing full well that this man was cut from the same pattern of Blake himself, and yet wondering if he were not exaggerating the man's potentiality simply because on first sight Hetherington spoke well and acted independently—and because he stood tall and strong on his two feet.

"Got your own truck?"

"That's right," Hetherington said. "Prefer to use my own."

There was nothing to say to that. The pickup was a shambles.

"Do as you like," Blake told him.

Luke saluted and turning away, announced that he was going to the stable to look over the horses.

The afternoon got hot close after three o'clock, and Luke stopped and passed a ragged handkerchief across his brow. It had been a long morning, with a short twenty minutes for lunch in the mess, and then back at the paddocks, watching each horse, marking it down, talking to the swipes and the grooms and memorizing their names and the things they said about Bel Aire. He had not seen Blake again, and Vince had told him that Blake got over-tired and had gone back to the house. He was satisfied that Blake had not interefered with him so far. Black's reputation as a horseman, hotheaded and proud, was an infamous one, and Luke had expected to have some trouble at first. The trouble would be worth it, he had decided, for Bel Aire was a fabulous dream for any man who loved horses, to breed them, to train them, to race them—there was no specialty at Bel Aire. Luke knew that. He knew that only at Bel Aire could he exercise his complete love for the horse.

He stuffed the handkerchief back in his pocket and went to the stall near the left of the paddocks. Vince was standing there, and in the inner dark Luke saw the handsome bay horse with his ears pricked sharply as he swung gracefully around to stare at the open doorway. The horse had big eyes, black and brilliant, and an air of tense, alert quietness that created a portentous effect.

"Is he quiet?" Luke asked.

"With those who know how to handle him," Vince said. "The only trouble is no one handles him but Blake."

Luke put his hand out and touched the horse's shoulders. The brilliant skin crinkled a little in apprehensive anticipation. Then the animal relaxed again.

"You're not thinking of riding him?" Vince said.

"I don't know. What's his name?"

"Boris," Vince told him. "Blake thinks we ought to sell him now."

"How old is he?"

"About seven years—seven years and four months. He's a temperamental creature. They raised him for stud purposes but he didn't answer."

"There are horses like that," Luke said. "Don't take to the mares for some reason. . . . He looks powerful."

"He's eaten up with it. You can't put *him* through the shafts. He won't stand it. He's fine and powerful, but he's got to be handled. Blake's the only man for it. Used to be, anyway."

The horse's ears were laid back and he seemed to be listening, his face averted.

Vince said, "He's made a break a couple of times. One of the rubbers took him on once and rode him wild back in the woods. He had his head smashed against a low bough. Damn near broke his skull. Another time he crushed one of the swipes against the side of the stall. Broke the kid's leg."

Luke drew nearer the animal and touched him again. Boris seemed to drift away from him, ducking his head, and looking sideways at him from his shining black eyes. Luke put his hand on his side and stroked him. He stroked the animal's shoulder and the tense arch of his neck. He was almost slippery with hot, electric passion.

"I'm going to take him out," Luke said. "Cool him off some."

He swung himself up on the beast's back and gave a clucking sound. Boris went off at a slow, gentle trot, around the paddocks and through the gate. Once outside and on the clay path, he turned his head half around and made a whining noise, flung out a little foam, and set off. Vince stood near the stall watching them go. From around the side of the stables Raol came, his hands in his pants pockets, his face bright with pleasure.

"No one rides like him," he said to Vince.

Vince looked down at the boy. "Do you ride?"

"Yeah," Raol said, "but not like him. No one rides like him."

"No one?" Jett said. The pair turned and saw Jett behind them. She had on her black gabardine habit, her black boots, and the black leather crop in her hand.

"Do you know Raol?" Vince asked her. "Hetherington's son."

Raol smiled and Jett said, "I heard he had a boy. Hello, Raol." Then, walking in front of him, she said to Vince, "Saddle Don't," and she walked ahead to the stall where she kept the horse.

For an accountant and general business manager, Vince thought, I sure get the duties of a swipe. He laughed at his own indignation, knowing that there was little other contact with Jett, and that he was grateful for the chance to saddle the horse, and stand close beside Jett when she mounted.

"You're not going after him?" he said.

"Not *after* him, no! In the same direction."

She jerked the reins and kicked her spurs in the animal's side gently.

"You'll never catch up!" she heard Raol promise as she took off through the paddock gate.

Two hours later, the sun setting, Luke Hetherington cut up from the cliff path above the quarry and started back. It had been a good two hours, and the horse was a good horse, fast when he was supposed to be fast, and slow and obedient when that was demanded. For a reward, Luke had taken him down to the plains near the quarry and let him play in the green grass and drink his fill of the water there. Now he ran him along the road and the horse was bathed with perspiration, but screaming with delight in his equine way, scattering foam and pebbles to left and right. Toward the break in the wood path he heard the hoofs of another horse, and clearing to the side, he waited for the horse to pass, but it did not. Instead it came slower when it neared him, and he turned to see the girl riding almost alongside him.

He slowed the horse and nodded.

"Hello," she said.

"Hi."

"You manage the horse well."

"He's got spirit," Luke said, "but he's obedient to a good hand."

"And you're a good hand?"

"I expect I am."

"With other men's horses."

"The man who rides this fellow is laid up. Horse needs exercise."

"I should think," Jett said, "that would be up to the man who owns him."

Luke did not say anything to that, but wondered who the girl was. She was a beautiful girl, and the horse under her was beautiful too and familiar. He could not remember what he had been told about this Bel Aire horse when he had gone through the stables with the groom, but the horse was not the kind a man could forget. Black and sturdy and anxious to run, Luke could tell, by the eager way he jerked his head up when he was walking along that way. The girl was probably someone from town, out for exercise, or maybe it was the girl's horse, and she boarded him on the farm.

"You didn't answer my question," she said.

"I didn't know it *was* a question."

She had a special arrogance about her, a well-bred pride that was not typical of what Luke expected from a female raised in these parts; her beauty wasn't typical, either.

"And you don't know who *I* am, either, do you?" she said.

"Sorry, I don't."

"My name is Jett," she said. "Jett Black."

Luke wanted to laugh at the look on her face. She looked as though she had expected a royal trumpet blast to follow her announcement, or a majestic blow on a huge gong.

Instead, he smiled and said, "Pleased to meet you."

He had thought she would be much younger from Vince's description of Luke's daughter. Vince had said she was a little rebel but a good kid, and this was a woman, a spoiled, haughty female with an air of flamboyant disdain.

She said, "That's Blake's horse. You may be right, Mr. Hetherington, in saying that he will need exercise, but it's presumptuous on your part to ride him without asking Blake."

"Too late now," Luke said, "but I gathered from what Vince said that Blake'd find trouble getting an exercise boy for this fellow."

"Vince overestimates his danger."

"You ride him?"

"I could."

"Want to switch?"

She hesitated, and her horse jerked again in a restless gesture at being forced to stand there. His eyes seemed to spark a sudden decision and determination in her and she looked squarely at Luke.

"All right," she said, raising herself on her left leg to swing off the gelding's back. Luke jumped down and held Boris while she mounted. Then, going around behind her horse, he swung himself into the saddle and looked at Jett.

"The stable isn't far," he said. "Race?"

"Yes. Race!" she answered, and there was an immediate clucking sound from her as she moved the horse to action.

He started off fast, the horse she rode, and his canter broke into a speedy gallop and then faster, ahead of Luke. Luke dug his spurs into the horse's sides, not enough to hurt him, but to excite him, and the dust from Boris's hoofs met his face as Luke rode into it at a wild pace. He was gaining speed, but before he overtook them he could see the dust clearing and Jett swaying uneasily on the horse's back as though he were out of control.

"Hold him in!" Luke yelled. "Be his boss!" But she seemed not to hear, and Boris went like fury down the clay road, and then off, onto the bank of the fields in the clearing, going right for the white fence until he was almost on top of it. Instantly he planted his forelegs down firmly like a car stopping abruptly, the hind wheels of it skidding and throwing it sideways, and the arresting movement caused Jett to bolt forward in the air and land hard on the ground, her shoulders hitting the sod first.

Luke caught up to them and pulled Don't to a stop. He nearly fell off the gelding trying to reach the girl promptly, and when he leaned down to help her to her feet, she slapped his hand away and got up slowly unassisted. Boris was standing at the fence, passively, his breath coming in great heaves, his ears back. Jett looked at him and then back at Luke. She rubbed her forehead uncertainly.

"That was rough," Luke said. "Hurt?"

She did not answer, but walked straight to her own horse, Don't, and mounted, uneasily at first, as though she were badly shaken, and then, with great effort, she sat straight on the back of the animal.

"He's probably not used to a woman," Luke said. Inside he was laughing now that he knew she was all right. It was humorous to see the personal defeat written so angrily across her young, fine face.

"I'm not interested in your comments, Mr. Hetherington," she said.

"Look, it's nothing to get so upset about." He grinned at her and started to walk over toward her horse. "I've been thrown lots of times."

She made her horse back away from him. "*I* haven't," she said, studying him momentarily, the anger fresh in her eyes. "Don't take that horse out again until you have my father's permission."

"I'd be likely to give you that advice, Miss Black."

"You'd be more likely to follow my instructions," she said, "or maybe you want to learn that the hard way. I'm willing to make it plenty hard, Hetherington," she added, "plenty hard!"

A small fragment of hard-packed mud kicked up in Luke's face from her horse's hoof as it took off. He watched her go until she was a mere stick figure heading in toward the gate to the stables, and then, turning to pat the tired stallion's neck, Luke burst into a fit of shaking, uncontrollable laughter.

Chapter Seven

J ETT PULLED her jodhpurs off and examined the bruises
on her thighs. Her shoulders ached where they had struck
the ground, and the ache penetrated through to her back
when she sat up and moved about. She knew she should
have walked the distance from the spot where she fell to
the stable, but she could not give Luke Hetherington the
satisfaction of seeing her incapacitated. She hated him, his
intruding manner and his calm insolence, and she hated
herself for the spectacle she had made riding Boris. Standing up, she walked to the mirror and inspected her
bruises once more before she reached in the closet for
the wool robe. It was close to ten o'clock in the evening,
and Vince would arrive soon to help Blake get ready for
bed. When Blake had first told her that Vince was going
to perform these duties, a violent protest had run through
her mind, but she had checked the words she wanted to
say. It was proper for Vince to dress and undress Blake,
and she realized that the rebellious part of her nature
that damned propriety was selfish and foolish. The
thought that Blake might never have been paralyzed had
she not opposed his attempts to send her to college made
her sick inside. He was strong and fine, she knew, and
the weakness he had, he fought. But Jett could not fight
the weakness in herself, nor could she recognize her love
for Blake as a weakness. It was her strength, and her life's
blood, and it took courage for her to admit to convention
and to allow it to take its course in that house.

She hurried to fasten the robe about her and slip into
her scuffs. Quickly she ran a comb through her hair and
touched the lipstick to her lips. Then she opened the
door and went down the hall to the living room, where
Blake sat in an easy chair facing the picture windows, the

smoke from his cigarette making hazy blue curls in the
air.

"Bunny?"

She went around to the front of the chair and knelt on
the hassock.

"Hello, honey."

"What were you thinking?"

He stubbed the cigarette in the ash tray on the small
end table. "I'll be going to Richmond in another week.
Vince is going to drive me up there to see a doctor I heard
about. I guess I was thinking about that."

"Richmond! Wonderful! I can get some shopping done.
Bunny, we haven't been to Richmond in years!"

He shook his head and reached out to take her hand.
Her face had broken into that childish expression of joy
which he had been so fond of in the past when he had
surprised her on her birthday, or brought a gift to her
from one of his trips to Lexington.

"You can't go this time, Cricket," he told her. "Just
Vince and I. We'll only be gone a few days, and I think
you'll be helpful around the track. You know the pro-
cedure better than most, and Hetherington will need
help."

"I *hate* Hetherington," she said flatly.

"Jett, why be so dogmatic about the man? That's not
like you."

"I met him today," she answered, omitting the part
about riding Boris. She knew Blake was opposed to her
riding the horse, considering him too dangerous for her.
"In fact, I met him while he was riding Boris."

"He can handle the beast? Good!"

"What's good about it, Bunny? You'd think it was *his*
horse. In fact, you'd think Bel Aire was his farm."

"Well, he may seem headstrong. I think he's a good
man, though, honey. We need a strong man around here
now, and I think he's the one."

"We don't get along."

"Does he know that, or is that *your* idea?" Blake chuckled and reached for another cigarette. Jett stopped his hand. "Doctor's orders," she said. "Not too many."

"I think you enjoy bossing me, Cricket."

She held his hand tight and looked at him. "I enjoy taking care of you, Blake. I want you to get better—so much!"

He squeezed her hand and winked at her. "Thanks, honey," he said, and then, leaning back, "Now, what's all this about Hetherington?"

"I don't know exactly. I guess it's just that I'm used to your being the master. I don't like to see anyone in your place, Blake. It's silly, isn't it? But he's the kind of person that will try to take your place—try to take Bel Aire away from you."

Blake laughed. "He can't do that. You know he can't."

"If he were someone like Vince, someone you could trust . . ."

"Vince is a businessman, not a horseman. You'd never catch Vince on Boris' back!"

"That's what I mean," Jett said. "That's just what I mean."

The bell rang sharply and Jett sighed. "I suppose," she said, getting up to let Vince in, "there's nothing *I* can do about it, except just give him enough rope. . . ."

When she left the room, Blake reached for the cigarette and struck a match to it. He shut his eyes and again he tried to make his toes move, to feel the muscles in his legs and the movement of his knees. But there was nothing. Only the dead weight, and the knowledge that it was as it should be, and as Dr. Sellers had said it would always be. Still, he thought, there have been countless invalids told the same thing, and among them, men who have since walked. He would walk, he knew it, and he would do it as soon as it was humanly possible. A delay was a year, perhaps, and there were not many years he could spare. It would take time to be himself again, and meanwhile, it was wise to have a man like Luke Hetherington managing Bel Aire.

Blake knew that Hetherington was not a man to take orders unless those orders coincided with his own special way of getting things done. He knew, too, that Hetherington would never have the patience and quiet tolerance that Vince had. But Hetherington was an individualist and a man who knew his horses, and in the position of manager he was ideal. A thought came to Blake's mind then, and he reproached himself for it. He had thought that it was a good thing too, that Jett disliked Luke Hetherington. He reproached himself for thinking that because he knew too well what his obsession for his daughter had cost him, and what it would cost him in the future if he could not temper it and eventually discard it. He took a long drag from the cigarette and blew a fat smoke ring toward the darkness outside the window. For the time being, he decided, he would try to keep Jett very close to him. He would indulge in his obsession for a little while longer. At least for as long as he was paralyzed.

The cabin was made of logs, one floor, three rooms. There was a fireplace in the center room, and before it a table set with two places, with a checkered cloth under the white plastic plates. There was no rugs on the floors of any of the rooms, but two wooden beds in the room to the left, a dresser, and a table. In the room to the right there were trunks and suitcases, a broken rocking chair, a saddle, and a boy's bicycle. Luke and Raol were sitting on the hearth in the center room, and Luke was watching six sausages fry in the black pan rigged up over the open fire. Raol whittled a block of wood down, the shavings dropping to the tile before he kicked them into the fire.

"She's a pretty good rider, too," he said suddenly, after he had been whittling for a long time without saying anything.

"Who?"

"Miss Black. I watched her go out after you."

Luke flipped the sausages over and held the pan back to the sticks. Raol was a sad little kid and Luke knew it. Whatever new place Luke took him, wherever they went together, Raol always remembered the women he had met. He would not mention them immediately, but he would remember them, and later he would speak of them, and Luke would know he had thought of them most of the day. Raol needed a mother badly, or he needed someone who could act as a substitute. But if it were left up to the boy to decide, he would pick the first girl he came close to—a girl like that Black girl. Her type, Luke thought to himself, would walk all over his little boy's heart, and more than likely would never know there was a heart there, and that it was beating in time with the steps she took and the breaths she breathed.

"Is she like Ma?"

"We've been all through that, Raol. We've been all through what your mother was like."

"I don't mind going through it," Raol said.

Luke shifted his weight as he crouched before the fire. He wiped his brow with the back of his hand and grinned down at the boy.

"Well," he began, and the boy stopped whittling, "your mother was short—no higher than from here to that window ledge—and slender as a flower."

"Her hair was the color of wheat, wasn't it?"

"Yep. And her eyes?"

Dimples came to Raol's cheeks and he laughed. "Were bluer than the sky and soft like the clouds in the sky. And she could sing!"

"Lord, yes!" Luke said. "She *could* sing!"

He remembered the way she sang, her voice low like a humming wind caressing him on a hot night when a breeze was prayed for. Luke could remember. He had met Frannie in a little Kentucky town up in the hills near

Hill Valley Farm, and after they were married they had lived in the cottage just off the limits of the farm. She was shy and gentle, with a natural grace and beauty, and she was always singing, so that after she died Luke could hear her songs ringing in his ears until he nearly went mad with grief. Raol was born a year after they were married, and it was two years later that Luke drove Frannie to Louisville and heard the doctor's verdict. Cancer, he said, and she had a year, he said, but that spring she was dead.

"And I used to get sung to sleep." Raol's voice shook the memory. Luke pulled the pan of sausages from the fire.

"You sure did, fellow," he said, forking them to the plates. "How about getting the applesauce from the freezer?"

They were sitting down at the table when the knock came at the door, and Luke shouted that it was open and to come on in. It was frightening to see him come through the door. He was too tall for the entrance, and after he stooped to avoid hitting the top ledge, he straightened again, but his head sat lopsided on his shoulders. When he smiled, his mouth had wide gaps where there were no teeth and the few teeth that showed were discolored and uneven. He was rubbing his giant-sized hands together and the roughness of his skin made a scraping sound.

"You Mr. Hetherington?"

"That's right."

"You want a man to drive fer yuh?"

"How'd you know?"

"Seen one of the swipes in town. He said you was thinkin' to hire a driver."

"Mostly for transporting the horses from here to Piedmont Junction."

"That's what I hear. All out-of-town jobs I hear it was."

"No, some of it will be local."

Willie shuffled his feet nervously. "I'm a good driver,

mister, and there's them that'll swear to it. I need the job, mister."

"Well, you were here first. Can't deny that. When can you begin?"

Willie's face screwed up in a frown. His tongue licked the corners of his mouth and he kept moving back and forth uneasily. "There's somethin' I—"

"What?"

"I thought it was all out of town. I didn't figure on the local, mister."

Luke said, "What's wrong with local? You live around here, don't you?"

"There's—Miss Black. She don't take to me. I was the one rammed her old—her father, and she don't take to me for that. I thought if it was out of town I wouldn't meet up with her and she wouldn't know, but I—"

"Wait a minute," Luke interrupted. "You mean you were involved in the accident?"

"Yes."

"Paper said Black was dead drunk."

"It don't matter. I git the blame anyways."

Luke dug into his sausage and stuck it into his mouth. Across from him, Raol had been quiet, eating and staring at the big figure of Willie Kane. Luke swallowed some water and looked back at Kane.

"You start tomorrow?"

"Yes, but you don't know, mister, what she'll say if she finds me—"

"I'm doing the hiring around here. What's your name?"

"Willie Kane, mister." His face was all mouth then, all smile. Luke nodded at Raol. "This is my son, Kane. Raol."

Willie's face got brighter and he looked foolish grinning down at the boy in that crippled manner of his, his huge body bending slightly to look at the boy. Raol returned the grin shyly, and Luke said, "O.K. See you tomorrow. Eight sharp."

Backing out of the door, Willie forgot to stoop and his head knocked on the wooden lintel above the entrance. He grinned harder and gave a low, coughy chuckle, and then, turning, he went out and banged the door shut behind him.

It was shortly after eleven before Raol went to bed. Luke shut the door to the bedroom and poked at the burning coals in the fireplace. From the table he took the old black bone pipe and emptied some tobacco into it, lighting it and smelling the tangy odor. He walked to the door and out on the path in front of the cabin. The mid-September air was still warm, but not hot, and there was some wind in the night. Luke walked along the path to the fields, and cut across to where the stables and the bunkhouses were. He listened to the noises, the Negro voices, the click of dice on the floor of the mess, and the leaves rustling in the trees. Rounding the corner, he met Vince Gellert.

"All settled?" Vince said.

"Pretty much so. Lot of junk to clean out of that spare room." They sat down on the log bench in front of the barn, and Vince yawned and crossed his feet in front of him.

"This is the nice time of the year. Early fall."

"Probably the quietest for business, too," Luke said.

"That's right. Good thing, too. Blake will start getting anxious come winter. Worrying about the yearlings and what not."

"I hired a driver," Luke said. "Came and asked for the job when I was eating dinner."

"Word goes like fire around here. Who'd you get?"

"Willie Kane's his name."

"No!" Vince sat up straight and looked at Luke. "He was driving the fruit truck that smashed Blake."

"He told me."

"And you hired the rascal?"

"It wasn't his fault, was it?"

"Not really, no. But you don't understand. You see,
Jett—"

"I understand about Jett. What about Mr. Black? He
got it in for Kane too?"

Vince thought a moment. Blake was always fair-
minded, rarely angry without cause. It was hard to know
what Blake would say, but he would listen to what Jett
said. Vince was sure of that.

He said, "I don't think it'll matter much what Blake
thinks. Jett hates Kane's guts."

"He drive good?"

"Sure, he drives all right. Dumb fellow, but all right
on the road."

"Then Miss Black will have to forget her grudge."

Luke's words had a dead finality to them, and Vince
wondered then just what he had expected Hetherington
to say. Hetherington was as bullheaded as Blake himself,
and as independent, too. He knew that, but he did not
know how Hetherington would cope with Jett. It was
obvious that he was not going to worry about her, not
in the least, and that from now on it would be a test
of wills at Bel Aire, with Luke's matched against Jett's.
For a perverse reason, Vince hoped that Luke would win
out, but for practical reasons he doubted it.

He said, "You play poker, Hetherington?"

"Some."

"There's a good game at the shed. The boys are fast and
it's best to bet light, but you'll learn a hell of a lot
of tricks. Want to join them?"

"Sure," Luke said. He stood and knocked his pipe
against the barn wall, rubbing out the ashes with the heel
of his boot. They went down the lane to the shed.

It was early morning, past one, before the game was
finished. Vince owed three and a half dollars to Shelly,
the cook, and Shelly and all the others were broke.
Luke Hetherington had a pocketful of change and a
whole wad of crumpled green bills.

Chapter Eight

Luke's truck was a big rambling wooden one, with a high front seat and a black tar roof to it. The horn had a thick, choking sound, and Willie pushed it and shook his head and chuckled.

"She old like a plow horse," he said, jumping down onto the fender and to the ground.

"We had that truck at Hill Valley." Raol was wringing out his towel back by the garage. He and Luke had come from their morning swim at the quarry, and he was barefoot, with only a pair of faded blue jeans on, held at the waist with an old colored tie that had been Luke's. His back was tanned deep and brown, and his neck and face were red from a fresh sunburn.

Raol looked up at Willie a long time, and then he said, "Is your head stuck?"

"That ain't no way to talk, sonny." Willie pouted, his big eyes looking down at the boy.

"I just wondered. I didn't mean anything."

"My head been this way since I was high as you. Before that, too. Always been this way."

"Couldn't you go to a doctor?"

"Ain't nothin' no doctor can do for Willie. Quit talkin' 'bout my head, boy. Bad enough."

"I'm sorry," Raol said.

"You and me gonna be friends, sonny." Willie fumbled around in his back pocket and brought out some chestnuts, holding them in his big hand. "Cut the meat out of these and make pipes," he said.

"How?"

"Punch a hole in 'em after they's hollow, and git a stick from a tree branch, and you got yourself a pipe to beat the band. You see if you haven't."

57

Raol reached for the chestnuts and turned them over to examine them. Again Willie fumbled in his back pocket, and this time he brought forth a knife, clicking it with his thumbnail so the blade sprang open. Then he stopped what he was doing suddenly and listened. He could hear her voice as she shouted to one of the men.

"Griselda's in foal," she was saying, and he could hear the steady step of her boots as she came closer. "I think we ought to separate her from the rest."

Willie jumped back, his eyes big with alarm.

"What you afraid of?" Raol asked.

"I don't want to see her. I don't want to see that one." He cringed there in the shadow of the truck, and Raol said, "It's only Miss Black. She's a good rider."

"Keep quiet, boy!"

"She won't hurt you, Willie," Raol said, and at that moment Jett could be seen coming around the corner and down toward the truck.

"Morning, Miss Black," Raol said. Willie sneaked down toward the front of the truck, but it was too late. She saw him, squatting up near the fender, his face wet with perspiration, the knife open in his hand. She brushed past Raol and went up to him, standing with her legs apart, her arms akimbo.

"You sneaking rat!" she said. "What are you doing on this land?"

"I was hired," Willie managed to say.

Jett screamed at him. "Liar! You crawling liar!"

"My dad hired him, Miss Black," Raol broke in. "He's telling the truth."

She turned and looked at Raol, then looked back at Willie Kane. "Hired!" She spat the word out. "Hired for what? To run around here with your open knife, you murderer? To kill around here?"

Raol said, "To drive the truck, Miss Black. He was just showing—"

"Get out of here, Raol! Stay away from this crazy man!

Hired! You maniac! I'll have you off this land in ten minutes, with a whip helping your legs go, I promise you."

She turned from him and ran back in the direction from which she had come. Willie's face was creased with fear, and there were round tears at the corners of his eyes. He began to cry, the tears rolling down and mixing with the perspiration and grease on his face, leaving long streaks down his cheeks. Raol stepped forward, leaned down, and picked up two of the chestnuts he had dropped when Jett had screamed at him. He walked over to Willie, who had now slumped down and was sitting on the ground, his head resting on the fender.

"She—she was m-mad at you," Raol said.

"She gonna git me, you see. She hates me."

"Aren't you going to run?"

"He said I could drive. You was there."

"He won't let her hurt you," Raol promised.

"What about *him*? Mr. Black? I don't know about him. Oh, Lord, I never had trouble like this. I need the job, sonny. I ain't got no money. Last night I slept in a field, I did. I slept in a cold field and the dew was all over me like it was on the weeds. I might as well stay in a field and let the tractors run over me and get digged up like the weeds."

"Don't talk like that," Raol said. "My dad will help you, Willie."

"Maybe, and maybe not," Willie said. He shut his eyes and brushed the wetness away from his face with his hands. The knife lay on the ground and he picked it up and stabbed the ground with it. "She thinks I'm crazy," he said. " 'Cause I'm ugly she thinks I'm crazy."

Once inside his office, Blake tossed the heavy mustard-colored blanket from his lap to the table, and pushing the wheels of his chair, he went to the desk. He shuffled some papers he found in the top drawer, picked up the silver pencil, and then turned his head toward the window and stared out It was a particularly clear day, the sun yellow and round in the high blue sky, and through the open spaces between the stables and the dirt trotting rings Blake could see patches of green grass, and the brown and yellow and orange coloring of the forests beyond He imagined himself on his feet, kicking the wheel chair aside, strolling and finally running out into that day, mounting the horse and riding with the fast freedom he knew so well His thumb pressed against the point of the pencil and the lead snapped and fell in a tiny piece to the desk top He wondered how many times he would engage in that dream before it was reality, and yet he never doubted that it would be real He could not afford that doubt

From around the white wooden fence the figure of Luke Hetherington strolled toward the walk His long arms hung out in defiance of the sleeves of his worn blue denim jacket, and the legs in his faded trousers took great steps, firm and easy on the ground below them The sand-white color of his hair was hidden by a round brown skullcap, and as he came closer Blake could see his lips pursed and hear the uneven, toneless whistling

Blake pushed the tab in the pencil, took the papers, and began making marks on them, his eyes turned away from the window and fixed on the desk At the sound of the knocking on his door he shouted, "Come on in," and feigned a busy interest in what he was doing

"Thought we ought to go over some things," Luke said He eased his thin body into the chair beside Blake's desk and took a pipe from his jacket pocket

"All right, go ahead " Blake dropped the pencil and swung his chair halfway to face him

"Vince told me you use Kaller for a vet," Luke said "I called him and he'll come next week He can check the animals for parasites and treat the weanlings Also handle the brood mares for pregnancy "

"You learn fast."

"Not much different setup here than Hill Valley." Luke sucked on the pipe and crossed his legs. "In two weeks I'd like to stud the Larkspur."

"Got a stallion in mind?"

"Great Neck, I was thinking of. He's by Bull Lea out of a Sir Galahad mare. Damn good combination."

"Exactly what I'd thought," Blake said. He could not help admiring Hetherington, and envying him too. After he got well, Blake decided, he would keep Luke on. The two of them would make a crack team, and there might be a good opportunity for expanding Bel Aire. As Luke talked further, Blake's enthusiasm for this idea grew, and he became impatient with his own physical condition. He made a mental note to start off for Richmond as soon as he could, and he would triple the pay of the doctor who cured him.

In the midst of Luke's talking the door flew open, and the two men looked up to see Jett standing before them. She was wearing the black jodhpurs and boots, and her blue shirt was tied at the waist, showing a small part of the smooth white flesh between the belt and the shirt's knot. Her black hair was piled on top of her head, and her eyes were hard and filled with obvious ire.

"What's the trouble, Cricket?"

She glared at Luke Hetherington, sitting there comfortably, and then she looked at Blake and said, "Did he tell you who he hired?"

"Did *who* tell me?"

"Him," she said, moving her head to indicate Luke.

"I better take over from here," Luke said, but Jett prevented him from saying more.

She said, "Willie Kane!"

"What are you talking about, honey?" Blake turned his wheel chair so that he faced her.

"Willie Kane was hired to drive the truck!"

"You mean the one who—I hit?"

"That's right," Jett said, "the one who hit you."

Blake looked at Hetherington, who was nonchalantly blowing smoke up from his pipe.

He said, "Where'd you get hold of *him*, Hetherington?"

"He came to my cabin last night and asked for the job. He thought it was a long-distance run and he didn't want it when I told him it was local too. He was afraid of Miss Jett."

"He's got reason to be afraid," Jett said. "Good reason!"

"Vince told me he drove O.K. and I didn't see any reason not to hire the man. He needs work and we need a driver."

"Who the hell do you think you are?" Jett screamed.

Blake said her name loud, evident anger in his tone. When she was quiet no one spoke for a moment, and then Blake said, "You won't have any dealings with the driver, Cricket."

She looked at him, her eyes filled with disbelief. "I don't see how you can stand to think of him working for Bel Aire. Blake, I don't see how—"

Blake interrupted her. "I don't even know the fellow well. If he's a good driver—"

"All right, what if he is? *I* hate him! Isn't that reason enough? *I* hate him!"

Luke stood up and took the pipe from his mouth. His back was turned to Jett and he addressed Blake. "I think I'll run along," he said. "We can get on with our planning later."

He went as far as the door, past Jett, never looking at her, and with his hand on the doorknob he turned to Blake. "Shall I tell Kane to go ahead with his work?"

There was silence. Jett watched her father carefully, trying to catch his eye and show her violent protest in a look, but Blake answered then.

"Yes," he said, "and check on his license. He can bunk out with the mess boys."

When he was gone, Jett stood before Blake staring at him. She did not speak. She could not believe what she had heard. Never before had Blake crossed her like that, and now she could not believe that it had happened.

"I'm sorry, honey," Blake said.

"I don't understand you," Jett said slowly. "I don't want to understand this. What is this man? What is he doing to everyone around here? You'd think he was God." She crossed over to Blake and stood before him. "Bunny, I've never in my life seen you let another man boss you. I've never seen you let another man make decisions for you. Don't you know what's happening? This Luke Hetherington is going to steal everything you've built up around here. He's going to walk all over us, and you're going to let him."

Blake smiled. "You're making a dramatic incident out of a very commonplace thing, Jett. The man hasn't been here more than a few days, and you've made your mind up to hate him. Of course he's going to make decisions, and I'm going to let him make them. His decisions are good ones, and for a while I'll need a man as capable as this one. I'd really lose Bel Aire if I didn't have a strong arm directing things around here."

"Good decisions! What a laugh! I suppose hiring Willie Kane is a good decision! Willie Kane, the man who almost killed you in that wreck!"

"Jett, you're forgetting some of the facts." Blake sighed and pushed his chair over so that he could look out the window. The girl followed and stood behind him. Blake said, "It could have been any man on the road that day. I was driving like an ass, and any man could have hit me. Actually, I hit him. You know that. The papers told you what I didn't tell you, and you know it."

"The hell with the papers," Jett said. "I know that twisted moron for the fool he is. I'm telling you, he's a fool!"

Abruptly Blake turned his chair around and looked at

his daughter. "And I'm telling you," he said briskly, "that Luke Hetherington is in charge here until I walk again!" His voice softened. "Jett," he said, "I told you I have to go to Richmond next week with Vince to see the doctors. I don't want to worry about what's going on here. I've put my trust in Luke Hetherington, and I've always trusted you. I'm trusting you now—trusting you to act like a mature person, to forget the wreck and Willie Kane and all the insignificant little grudges that cause trouble. Will you do that for me, Jett?"

As she looked at his face, she saw the tired lines under his eyes, the flush in his checks, the wrinkles on his forehead. She realized that she was making it difficult for Blake, very difficult, and she felt ashamed of herself. It was not easy for Blake to relinquish even a small portion of his duties at Bel Aire to another man, and yet he was trying to do it gracefully.

"You're right, Bunny," she said. "I *am* a brat."

"A nice brat, nevertheless. . . . Now how about letting me get some paper work done?"

She leaned down and kissed his forehead, and a feeling of warm security came over her. Laughing, she pinched his cheek and promised not to interrupt for at least another two hours. Then she would come and take him to the house for lunch.

Before she left, Blake said, "Another thing, Cricket. Next week, after I go, Hetherington is going to stud the Larkspur. I want you to help him. All right?"

"All right," she answered, and she wished he had not asked her to do that. Because nothing, nothing ever could still her resentment for Luke Hetherington. Restrained, hidden, checked, or withheld, it would remain for as long a time as Blake remained in that wheel chair.

Chapter Nine

I T WAS A WEEK after, one morning when breakfast was
finished, that Vince came up to the house to get Blake
and set off for Richmond. They planned to be gone ten
days, and Jett had spent most of the night before pressing
Blake's clothes and packing them in the pigskin valise.
They were sitting at the small white wooden table in the
kitchen, finishing their coffee, when the bell rang and
Vince was there.

"We ought to hurry," he said, "and make time while
the day's young. Traffic will get heavy toward noon."

Jett squashed her cigarette in the saucer and stood up
to wheel Blake into the living room, but he said he
could do it by himself, and he put his hands on the wheels
and moved out of the kitchen and down the hall.

"Take good care of him," Jett said to Vince when they
were alone. "I've never been separated from Blake longer
than a week."

Vince said, "The time will pass. You'll be busy around
here. Aren't you going to service the Larkspur today?"

"This afternoon. I'm not looking forward to it."

"You really dislike him, don't you?" Vince said.

"Do *you* like him any better?"

Vince leaned against the wall and stuck his hands in
the pockets of his neatly pressed brown suit. His red hair
was combed well, and the white shirt with the plain
striped tie gave him a strange city look.

"I don't know, Jett," he said. "I can't fight with him on
how he does his job. He's an expert. I don't know. I
think I *do* like Hetherington, in a business way as well as
personally." As he said the words he wondered if the
only thing that kept him from being more enthusiastic
about Luke was the fact that Luke took over the work

at Bel Aire so masterfully. In less than a week he had set up his own schedule and put his own routine in practice, and it was as effective as it was brilliant. The workers liked him, too, Vince realized, probably more than they liked Vince. It was ridiculous to be jealous of the man, and yet Vince wondered what man could resist feeling that way. Blake could, perhaps, but then Blake had been his match, and fully expected to be so again when he recovered. Vince had learned to half accept Blake's dream of recovery, because he had never seen Blake lose a battle yet, and now, with Blake's determination fired double, Vince would not be surprised if Blake made a mockery of Sellers' conviction that the paralysis was permanent.

Jett called in to Blake to see if he needed help and he answered that he was ready. She heard the bang of the wheel chair against a wall as he made his way toward them.

"Don't forget," she said to Vince softly, "take care of him."

On his lap Blake had his hat and coat, and in the rack where his legs rested the heavy suitcase was balanced. Vince picked the suitcase up and started toward the door. When the screen banged shut, Jett bent down and kissed Blake on the cheek, and then lightly on the lips.

"I'll miss you, Bunny."

"You be good," he said, "Watch out for things while I'm away." He wanted to say more suddenly, and for a brief minute he wished she were going with them. It was better, he knew, that Jett stayed at Bel Aire, but there was so much love in him for her that he was rarely calm or at rest when she was not near. Ten days would be too long. In the past, his short trips to the races when the farm ran a yearling had seemed lengthy and tiring, and he had known that the reason was his absence from his daughter. When she began to grow up, well into her teens, he had sent other people in his place, or he had allowed her to cut school and make the trips with him.

Only in a few instances had they been separated after Jett's sixteenth birthday, nearly four years ago.

He looked at her and smiled, touching the back of her hand to his lips. Then he started the wheels turning, and Jett followed him to the porch steps, where Vince was waiting to lift him from the wheel chair into the front seat of the car. As he picked Blake up, the veins stood out in Vince's forehead, and his face became a deeper red than his hair. Somehow he managed to place Blake securely in the seat, and then, collapsing the wheel chair, he shoved it in the back of the car.

Again Jett bent forward and brushed her lips across Blake's cheek. She looked very sad, Vince thought as he waited to shut the door, too sad. Ten days was a short time, not the century Jett made of it. But as he thought that, he looked at Blake and saw that his face was a mask of grief too. As Dr. Sellers said, this pair was thick as thieves, Vince mused, and when he shook hands with Jett and bade her good-by he wished that even an eighth of the misery reflected in her dark eyes was caused by his own departure.

Driving down the road from the house, Vince could see Jett in the mirror. She was standing back by the side of the house watching the car go off in the distance.

Luke Hetherington was looking forward to the afternoon with as little enthusiasm as Jett. It was pointless to argue with Blake, to try to convince him that he was quite capable of servicing the mare himself. Blake had been adamant about Jett's assistance, and that was the end to the matter. Luke seldom thought of a woman as a bitch, particularly when she was as young a woman as this one, but for all his inner respect of womankind in general, he couldn't push aside the conviction that Jett Black wore a bitch label with big red letters on it. Perhaps that was what came of a girl who was fathered without ever knowing a mother, and if it was, Luke thanked God

that Raol was a boy. But he did not believe that that was
the whole truth of the matter. Even with a mother, it
would be hard for a girl to grow into a sweet, normal
woman when she had a father like Blake to spoil her.
He was glad that Blake upheld his decision to keep
Willie employed, and he realized the full significance of
Blake's concession.

Luke finished lunch and hunted for Raol, who was
preparing to go fishing. He checked over the boy's equip-
ment and sent him off in the direction of the quarry,
glad for Raol that he had an environment that gave him
every opportunity for youthful sports and games. Jiffy,
the cook's son, went with Raol, and Luke could not help
smiling as he watched the two small figures strut down
the dirt road, proud as kings. When they were out of
sight, Luke walked along the stable until he came to the
Larkspur's stall. Her name was Bella Donna. Patting her
nose, he turned when he heard the even sounds of footsteps coming, and he saw Jett then.

"Afternoon," he said, trying to scare up some form of
smile.

Her face too seemed frozen. She smiled a dull "Hello."

"You want to lead out Bella Donna? I'll bring Great
Neck around. Might as well take them in the left corral."

"All right," she said, striding up to the great mare.

Luke left them and went on to the barn where Great
Neck was waiting. He was a fine stallion, magnificent and
powerful, and Luke took his halter and talked to him as
he led him from the stall out into the sun and down
the path to the corral. By the post, he waited while Jett
took care of the mare.

In the corral, Jett let the mare walk around a bit, and
the mare kept lifting her head and sniffing the wind.
She caught the stallion's scent, and she was an excited
beast, eager and scared too, but never once losing her
dignity. Her eyes roamed around trying to locate the big
stallion, and Jett led her over to the little hole scooped

out in the middle of the corral for her hind legs. She
turned back and signaled for Luke to bring the horse in.

Great Neck was a mighty gray stallion, large and beautiful to see. He was excited too, Luke could tell, but
he didn't charge or rear or stamp the way some of them
did. He stood and looked at Bella Donna, and his eyes
were shining, intense and fiery. He began to breathe
hard, and Luke watched the sides of his chest moving
in and out, faster and deeper. Under his glossy gray coat
Luke saw the muscles of the stallion, strong and ample.

"Bring him on!" Jett said, and there was a smile on her
face now. She loved this work and it made her feel good
every time.

Luke said, "He's coming, don't worry."

Bella Donna knew he was there and she whinnied
softly, a tremor passing over her on down to the sides
of her legs. The stallion let the air rumble through his
flared nostrils in a heavy snort as Luke walked him
around the mare. Once in front of her, Great Neck
snorted again, tossed his head wildly, and shook his
mane.

"God!" Luke heard Jett say. "Look at them!" Her voice
was high in pitch and anxious in tone. It was hard not
to feel that way, Luke knew, because he could feel it in
himself. Anyone who loved horses could sense the earthy
beauty of the moment, know its natural passion, and bow
to its glory. He led Great Neck up from the side, and
Jett steadied the mare. She did not have to steady her
very long.

One of the grooms leaning on the fence screamed out
in delight, and Luke looked over his shoulder and saw
half a dozen standing by, watching. It was a great sight,
he knew, and they knew it was too. Jett was thrilled with
it, and standing beside Luke, she looked up once to
smile and share her feeling. When their eyes met, they
held the glance for longer than they both knew. The
smile faded from her lips and she just stood there looking

at him, a startled look in her eyes, and for a second
Luke did not know her any more, but only that she
was young and fair and her eyes had a deep beauty
to them.

Then there was another yip from the groom at the
fence, and Luke looked in time to see the stallion walk
slowly away. Luke followed the stallion, and at the gate
the big horse turned and looked back at the mare. Luke
could see Jett watching them, and he stood still and
looked back at her. She half raised her hand and waved
them off.

She stood there then alone. A boy had jumped the
fence and come over to take the mare away, and Jett
was still for a moment, her right foot with its boot toe
tracing circles near the hole where the mare's hind legs
had rested. She did not want to think, and she did not,
but felt the sun tearing at her back until she removed
her jacket and put it over her arm, and loosened the
scarf around her neck, and began walking very slowly out
of the corral.

One of the grooms shouted, "That was fine!" and she
smiled at him without answering, because it was so fine.
The two proud animals, she thought, coming together
like that, and then she let the train of thought slip by
because it would spoil it to rehash it that way.

She knew where she was going.

He was sitting on the three-legged stool inside the stall
of the stallion, wiping his face with his shirt, his chest
bare and the wetness streaked on his skin from the sweat-
ing in the heat. Jett stood in the entrance a few short
seconds before he saw her.

"Mr. Hetherington," she said, "I think we'll have a
colt."

He laughed. "You and me?"

The exercise boy had taken Great Neck to pasture and
there was only the flat matted part in the straw in the
stall where the stallion had spent the night. Luke got

up and pushed the stool back toward the straw and reached for the sponge in the water bucket on the floor. He squeezed it and let the water run on him, his forehead and cheeks and neck and chest, until it splashed down and made damp stains on his tan pants.

She said, "I learned more from horses than I did from any teachers or any people at all."

He patted his wet face with a ragged towel, and wished she would go away. She annoyed him with this performance, completely reversing his previous opinion of her. Now she had soft lines to her face, a wistful expression, and she hung around there in the stall and it made him nervous.

"Yes," he said "you're right. Time I got busy with *my* lessons. I expect the vet will be coming soon and I ought to get the brood mares lined up."

From a hook on the wall he took a cotton T shirt and pulled it over his head. With his hands he slicked back his light hair, but it shot back up again in tiny points.

Suddenly she took a step nearer to him. "You keep your distance, don't you, Mr. Hetherington?"

"What do you mean by that?"

"I mean you're always just cool-warm. You don't run hot and cold."

"You talk riddles," he said, reaching down to pick his watch up from the stool, "and I haven't got time for them." He straightened and looked at her. "From the first day we met you made it pretty clear about distance and temperature."

She said, "I thought I was making something clear now."

He kept looking at her. "Maybe you better say what you mean, ma'am," he said.

For the first time her eyes left his face and traveled the full length of his tall, thin body to the toes and then back up to his eyes, and he was sure then what she meant. He put his hand out without stretching for her at all, and pulled her to him, his lips on hers hard, with scorn in his heart in the beginning, then wonder, then mere force when he felt her body slacken. They stayed that way until his hands dropped and he stood close to her, but not touching her now, only watching her eyes open, her feet get more steady under her, a look of bewilderment change to quick shock on her own face.

Then he wanted her. Before he had not, but then he wanted her, and his hands came to her shoulders again but she pulled away and stepped back, her eyes getting darker, the full red lips trembling uncertainly.

She took another step away from him.

"Wait!" he said, and the sharp command brought her lips together, pressed hard and firm, making her chin look tight. The flash came back in her eyes, and with one last glance she turned to go.

He said, "Wait!" and his long arm reached out to hold her but caught only the frayed end of her white neck scarf, and he stood with it in his hands, and he knew she was running from the sounds of her boots on the dirt path outside the barn.

Chapter Ten

THERE WAS no moon. The sky had a strange gray cast to it as Luke walked from the cabin, and there was a fresh damp smell to the air, a warning of eventual sudden rain. It was after eight o'clock, and Luke could see the cook through the mess windows, hear him singing out a lusty spiritual in high, drunken tones, slamming the dishes into the steaming water while Jiffy sat on the high wooden stool, slapping his knees and laughing when his father came to the chorus of hallelujahs. Raol had been exhausted after his full day's fishing in the hot sun, and he was asleep back in the cabin. Luke wondered if *he* would ever sleep that night.

He walked down by the paddock and climbed up on the fence, taking his pipe from his pocket and stuffing it with the yellow pieces of dried tobacco. After he touched the tobacco with the flame of the match, he watched the smoke drift out in the night air, pointing itself in wavering lines up in the direction of the house. The wind was blowing that way, and it was a restless wind. Luke looked at the distant box shape standing on the hill, and he saw the bright lights shining from the square windows. She was alone, he knew that, and he wondered why she had all the lamps burning that way, and what she was doing.

The afternoon had not been a revelation to Luke. Jett Blake had not reversed her pattern after all, he reflected. Spoiled, domineering, she had used the only weapon she had left to spear Luke's resistance in her quest of power over men—her body. And the surprise in her eyes? Luke laughed when he remembered the genuine shock registered there. The answer was simple. She had never had to depend on her physical ammunition before, and she was amazed and frightened at the result. Luke had

73

never trusted a bold, aggressive woman who was afraid of passion at the showdown, and he thoroughly mistrusted Jett Black. He could reason out everything in his own mind, explain all that had happened, and understand all that was necessary to understand about the girl, and he had done that hours ago. Yet he was still thinking about her. In a sense, she had challenged him, and he wondered if he would accept her challenge.

It would take only a few hours, at the most, and it would involve a long walk up that hill. The rain would come soon. In his back pocket, the white scarf was stuffed carelessly, and reaching for it, Luke shook out the wrinkles and felt the soft silkiness of the material. He looked up at the clouds and debated with himself momentarily, and then, tossing the scarf in the air and catching it in his hand, he stood up and started to walk toward the house.

The thunder cracked across the air, and the lightning darted in through the window in a sudden flash. Jett put the book down and ran back to the kitchen to close the screen blinds. She turned on the heat under the coffeepot on the stove and stood waiting for it to get hot. It was useless to read anyway, she thought, and she could not recall anything she had read while she was sitting in the living room. Since she had first entered the house late that afternoon, she had not been able to stop thinking about Luke Hetherington. Her mind was haunted with a realization of the meaning of the kiss she had given him. He was a mere stranger, but the kiss, the feeling she had experienced in that interval of their being together—that was not strange. It had a fierce familiarity that rang in her brain and made her remember. She hated Luke Hetherington for that, hated him with a violence that she could feel in her limbs as she stood in the kitchen. The coffee boiled and Jett turned the flame off, took a cup from the rack, and poured the brown liquid into it. She carried the cup to the front room.

The living room was immense and modern, with straight lines, simple well-cut furniture, and sparse decoration. It was a man's room, a fine rich one done with elegant restraint. Jett walked over to the broad green divan and set the cup on the triangular glass coffee table. She sipped the coffee, listening to the wind outside as it pushed the rain against the house. Her mind tried to focus on her actions from the time she had helped Hetherington with the servicing until the time she had gone to him in the barn. The thoughts emerged in a jumble of meaningless instances, like the fragments of a stale dream that were impossible to reassemble. The dream was a nightmare, and no nightmare had ever shaken Jett to this extent.

When the doorbell rang, she knew who it was.

She did not answer. Lightning danced in the black sky from the window she was facing. The rain seemed to come harder, and the wind was stronger. Again the bell rang out, and a fist beat on the kitchen door.

Jett was not afraid. Instead, she felt a pleasing contempt and scorn for his presence there. She heard his voice and the hammering sound of his heavy knocking as he repeated her name, and she smiled.

It vanished immediately. The door at the kitchen burst open, and she listened to the thud of his feet as he walked across the linoleum floor, the door slamming behind him. His footsteps softened as they met the hall rug, and she knew he was coming into the room where she sat waiting. He stood there then, holding the sopping white scarf in his hand, his eyes glaring at her.

"You don't answer your bell, but you leave your door open," he said. "That shows an odd twist in your thinking, Miss Black!"

The words were snarled. He flung the wet white scarf at her, and it landed on the table in a soggy heap. Jett stared at him, but anything she might have said remained clogged in her throat.

His light hair was pasted to his head in flat wetness, and the dirty white work jacket he wore was dripping. His trousers were drowned and muddy at the cuffs, and his shoes were caked with mud. The rug underneath him was drenched with puddles of water. He wrenched his long arms free of the jacket, swinging it over the back of a chair.

"It's going to rain for a couple of hours," he said. He looked at her, his eyes impassive and even as they passed over her. She did not look frightened or surprised, but alert now, and mean. The brown sweater she wore was tucked into a gray flannel skirt, and her bare legs were drawn up under her on the divan. A pair of brown loafers lay at the foot of the table.

She said, "Get out!" and Luke laughed at her.

He sat down in the chair where his jacket hung, and he pulled his muddy shoes up, reaching for the laces, undoing the knot and pulling his feet from the soaked leather.

"You'll be fired for this," Jett said.

"For what?"

"For coming here. You know damn well!"

"You asked me to come," he said. "*You* know damn well!"

When his shoes were off he leaned back in the chair and snapped off the light at his side. The built-in lights near the fireplace gave a quiet illumination to the room, and outside the jerky streaks of lightning dashed across the blackness.

Jett put her coffee on the table, and he was watching her. She met his glance and held it.

"Don't underestimate Blake," she said. "He'll kill you, I promise you that."

"He'll run over me, I suppose."

She swore at him, and her hand hit the cup, knocking it to the floor, where it rolled listlessly on the rug under the table. Luke Hetherington got up and bent down to pick up the cup. He put it back on the table and stood before her, his hands in his pockets.

Jett's eyes left his face and went down to the pockets of his trousers. She heard him snicker, and she looked away. When she looked back, his hands were at his sides, his fists tight. His face was drawn, cold in its appraisal of her, firm in desire, the cheeks sunken, the lips pulled down, set. She jumped to her feet and stood, her arms thrown back, her fingers spread apart. Luke did not move. A vein of his neck rose, beating, and fell down again.

Then he reached for her. He held her, and she felt the bones of his arms clamp across the bones of her ribs. Her legs kicked tight against his knees, and his mouth came on hers like fire.

In the first instant, in the shock of his skin against hers, she lay still in his arms, and then a knife of terror cut through her and she thrust her elbows at his throat, twisting her body to escape. Her fists came down on his face, hard blows, and loosening her fingers, she let her nails dig into his flesh. With one hand he took her two wrists and pinned them at her waist, wrenching her shoulders. Her head bent back, and she could feel him rip her sweater at the neck. The wool was tough and unyielding but it ripped there at the neck. She tore herself free.

Jett fell back against the chair, her eyes wide with fear, crouching there watching him. The amusement was evident in his face and she realized that he had let her go intentionally. His large body stood before her, legs apart, arms hanging at his sides, and there was a fresh trickle of blood running down his cheek. He let her wait, and she did, not screaming, not talking, not even whispering. Then he came toward her again, lifting her easily, smiling. He threw her down on the divan, and she felt the hatred, the helpless, horrible hatred for him seep through her veins.

She was able to say, "No!" before she fell back, his hand holding her while his other hand pulled the sweater roughly over her head. She stopped struggling momentarily while she caught her breath and let her strength come back. Then she was fighting him again, but less fiercely now, and suddenly not at all. Her arms dropped away from him, and she felt the downy texture of the divan and closed her eyes, spinning, spinning. . . .

She heard him say, "That's better. That's better, isn't it?"

She heard her own voice cry, "Yes!" and then she lay still.

Suddenly she was glad. Suddenly she felt free, light, happy. He was still now, and they did not talk. His breathing came heavy and she shut her eyes. A short smile stayed on her lips.

Luke woke up. The clock on the shelf across the room read eleven. He felt that he had been asleep for hours, but it had been only a short while. She lay beside him, her body beautifully relaxed, her cheeks flushed with a deep, peaceful sleep. The rain raged outside, and Luke listened to it. He got up, looked down at her, and covered her with her own clothing. His shoes were still damp and he squeezed his feet into them. Holding his jacket in his hand, he stood over her once more, moving the skirt up to cover her breasts. There were three switches on the wall and he fumbled with them until he found the one that would turn off the built-in lights and leave the room dark. She did not awaken as he slipped out the kitchen door and went hurriedly through the rain down the hill.

Behind him, a figure in the bushes crept along, following him. Luke hurried and the thunder pounded out. The figure in the bushes did not attempt to pursue him further when Luke broke into a run. It remained behind at a distance, crouching there halfway on the hill, and

when the light jagged out violently overhead, Willie
Kane covered his eyes and cursed the wild night.

The telephone rang out.

Jett heard it, but she lay unmoving on the divan. It
rang again and again, persistently, and she opened her
eyes and stared into the darkness of the room. She remembered now.

The ringing kept on.

Frantically Jett ran across the room, feeling her way in
the darkness, reaching on her knees for the neck of the
phone and lifting it to her mouth.

"Hello!"

She switched on the light on the table, and saw her
own nakedness with horror. She turned it off again.

"Hello, Jett? Jett?"

"Yes."

"Jett, it's Blake!"

"Yes, Blake." Her words were matter-of-fact. Everything was coming back to her.

"Honey, you sound funny."

"I'm—I'm all right."

"Cricket, what's the matter? What's the matter with
you? Were you asleep?"

"Yes, I—I was asleep."

She wondered how long ago Luke had left. Her body
was spent and she could not think. She tried to concentrate, tried to believe it was all real.

"Poor baby," Blake was saying, "I woke you up. I've
been trying to get you but the circuits have been busy.
Storm and all, I guess."

"How are you, B-Bunny?" she managed to say.

"I really got you out of slumberland, didn't I, Cricket?"

Jett felt hysterical. *Slumberland!* he said. She wanted
to cry.

"Bunny," she said, "when are you coming home?"
More than anything she needed him now, she told her-

self. Kneeling there on the floor of that room, she wanted his strength, his presence, his assurances.

"Ah, that's my girl. Well, look, honey, it'll only be a day or so after all. The checkup will take one full day and I may not get any reports on it right away, but I want to wait and see if I can't hurry them up."

"Please do, Blake. God, Blake, I—" She resisted the desire to blurt it all out. "I miss you," she said flatly.

"You sound pretty lonesome. Don't be depressed, Jett. I'll be back soon, and if we're patient, one day I'll be able to ride with you again."

The muscles in her legs pained her. She shifted her position and sat up on the chair, but that hurt her too.

"How's everything going there?" Blake asked.

"Fine. Fine, it couldn't be better."

"You and Hetherington getting along all right?"

The tears rolled down her cheeks then. "Yes," she said. "Yes."

"Did you service the mare? Did it go all right?"

She said "yes" again, and the tears were falling faster, running down her cheeks and splashing onto her breasts.

"Well, look, honey, I won't keep you up. You go back to bed now and get a good night's sleep. I'll be in touch with you."

"Come home soon, Bunny," she was able to say, and then, weakly, "Good-by."

She let the phone fall back in its cradle, and she fell back down on her knees. She wanted to crawl like an animal to the divan and climb up on it, but she could not. Her body shook with sobbing and each sob hurt her, until, giving in, she fell flat on her stomach, crying out in the darkness.

Chapter Eleven

The pillow dropped on Luke's head and awakened him. He brushed it aside and opened one eye. Raol was standing by the bed grinning.

"It's seven-thirty," he said, "and I want to see the pony!"

The sunlight from the window made Luke blink, and he sat up, stretching and yawning, shaking himself to consciousness. He had slept well. This was the morning he had promised Raol the pony, his first horse, and it had arrived from Lexington late last night.

"I got the coffee on," Raol told him. "Hurry up!"

Luke's hand reached for his pants on the chair beside the bunk, and when he felt them, they were damp. He got up and went across to the closet, where he found his overalls and a tan shirt, and he dressed fast, slipping into a pair of sneakers without bothering to put on socks. There was water in the basin on the bureau and he splashed it over his face and through his hair.

In the other room, Raol had the coffee poured into the white mug, and he was reaching in the oven for toast.

"You're on the ball this morning, son."

He eased himself into the chair at the table and the hot coffee tasted fine. Raol shoved the toast in front of him, chewing off a hunk of a piece he held in his hand, and with his mouth full he said, "Woke up last night in the middle of the storm. Where were you, Pop?"

"I had some business to take care of. Swallow what you're eating before you try to talk."

The boy swallowed and took a drink of water. He said, "Were you getting the pony settled?"

"I haven't seen him yet myself. We'll see him for the first time together."

"Were you playing poker?"

Luke shuffled his feet under the table and put the mug to his lips. Raol was not afraid to be alone at night, he knew that, but he felt guilty at having left the boy when they were so new to Bel Aire. Still, the child had to stand on his own feet.

"I was taking care of a mare," Luke answered him. He could not help thinking that there was a lot of truth to what he had said. There had been no more to it than that, and there would be no second meeting if Luke could help it. The matter was finished. He finished the coffee and Raol handed him his skull cap. Together they left the cabin and walked up toward the barn. Last night's rain had left the air clear of dust, and it was fresh, with a warm fall sun to make the day bright. Raol ran ahead, waiting at the barn door while Luke caught up with him and slipped the latch, rolling the door back and walking in. The pony was in the third stall, and Raol let out a yip of delight when he saw him. He had a rough chestnut coat with a tangled mane, and his ears were forward. His eyes were nervous, and there was a hint of disobedience in them.

Raol said, "He needs a good currying. When can I ride him?"

"Not yet," Luke said. "He's not even halter-broke yet." He reached for the brush and currying comb from the wall, and took down the barrier of the box stall. "Come on," he said to Raol. "Get to know him."

Raol put his hand out gingerly and touched the horse. The pony's eyes got fiery and he shifted to a kicking position, but Luke stroked his neck and said, "Eeeee-zy!" and the pony relaxed while Luke curried him.

After the hair was piled there in the stall Luke said they ought to let him run. He pushed the barrier aside and they stood watching the pony. At first the animal did not move, but whinnied softly and then shrilly. Luke gave him a gentle push and the pony went. Racing down

the barn, into the corral, he galloped in circles, jumping
forward and coming down on stiff legs. Raol and Luke
ran after him, watching from the gate of the corral, and
he was a scared beast. He stood still for a moment,
quivering, his ears stiff and his eyes white. Then he
walked to the water trough, snorting and burying his
nose in water up to his nostrils. Luke saw him and knew
he was a good horse, a horse with spirit.

In the bedroom, Jett stood at the window. The towel
was wrapped around her waist, and her face was still
moist from the scalding bath she had taken. She still
felt dirty and tired and sick. It was hard to forget the
way morning had come. She had awakened with a chill
there in the living room. A few inches from the divan
there was a dried spot of mud left from his shoes, and
beyond that, her ripped brown sweater, and her skirt and
underclothes strewn about. A sudden surge of nausea had
swept through her, and she had pulled herself up and
run to the bathroom. That was the way morning had
come, and the thought of the night kept her sick in-
termittently until now, as she stood looking out at the
hills and the stables. Now she was spent, physically and
mentally.

She was plain afraid. Here was a man who had loved
her as a man will love a woman, and yet he was strong
and calm and aloof. She could not command him or
break him or bend him to her will because he had no
reason to fear her, no reason to respect her or love her.
He was a man who met her in a contest of personalities,
and he had won the first time out. He had sized her up
well, determined her vulnerability, and acted accordingly,
and the result was his victory. Jett vowed that he would
not be victorious again, and she knew that the only way
to prevent it was to end the contest. She would make it
clear that it was over. When she met him, she would be
poised and distant, and she would not let him remember

what she herself could not possibly forget. That it had been good. That it had been significant and powerful and good.

As she dressed she remembered the way Blake's voice had sounded on the phone, concerned and apologetic for disturbing her sleep. If he had known what had preceded that sleep, she knew that it would be her own suicide. Because Blake was her life, and it would kill him to know. She thought of Blake's threat months ago to send her to college, to get her away from him so that she would be normal, and she knew the shallowness of that threat, the empty conviction behind it. There had been times for her too—times when she realized the consequences of their love for one another—but the realization did not stifle the feeling. The love between them was like a living tree that grew off somewhere away from the sun, faced with the wind and the unchecked assaults of the elements, but growing despite that, growing well and beautifully. She smiled at her own analogy. Weeds grow that way too, she thought.

She combed her long black hair and let it hang free at the shoulders of her crisp white blouse. The zipper at the side of her jodhpurs stuck, and she pulled at it until it fastened. Then, sitting on the bed, she tried to fit her boots on her feet, and the pain came back along her shoulders where Luke's hands had held her. Another wave of depression enveloped her, and she lay back staring up at the ceiling, one boot on, the other kicked under the bed. Closing her eyes, she relived the whole evening, the words he had said, the way his face had looked when he said them, the force he had used when he thrust her on the divan, the struggle, and then the slow, steady genesis of her own passion. Her whole body shook, and she heard a sound that came from somewhere within her, and it was the dry, short sound of a sob, but she was not crying. Her eyes were not wet, and there was only that sound coming and going, and the shaking.

At noon the sun was hot and the day was a scorcher. Luke had a yearling out near the paddocks, holding it by a halter shank while the swipes stood by to aid the breaking. One of the smaller swipes boosted himself on the yearling's back to get him used to saddle weight, and the animal reared and kicked while Luke held the shank hard. He saw her then, when he turned quickly to prevent the beast from bucking. She was standing by the fence watching. He did not like her being there, though he knew she had the right, and he called time and told the boys to get some lunch. They led the yearling away, and Luke went off to the mess. He did not look back at her or give any indication that he had seen her.

She watched him go. The fear subsided and she was glad that he had not noticed her. She wanted to see him again, just to look at him, because she knew that would be the first step. Once she had seen him, she thought, the nervousness and the embarrassment would pass, and they had passed. Watching him work like that, she was able to return him to his rightful place in her mind. He was an employee, a horseman who worked for her father, and she promised herself she would concentrate on that until last night was wiped out. If he had turned and looked at her, she did not know how she would have reacted. But now she did not have to worry. She would stay clear of him.

She walked to the brick building where Blake's office was. He had instructed her to watch the mail and pass along the important correspondence to Luke. If there was anything there, she could place it in Luke's box while he ate, and she would avoid contact with him.

The desk was cluttered with papers and letters. On the top of the heap there was a wire and she ripped it open. It was from Blake. He would be away for two days longer. She sat down in the swivel chair and opened the other envelopes. Her disappointment prevented her from making sense of their contents, and she pushed them all

aside and sat still. Two days to wait for him, and meanwhile she would not help Hetherington. Jett told herself that she should be glad for those days if they were
to make Blake well again, and after he got well again,
she planned to convince him that they both needed a
vacation. Luke Hetherington would not be needed when
Blake got on his feet, and there would be no more
problems. She would go off somewhere with Blake, and
when they returned, Hetherington would be gone and
the cabin empty.

Her shoulders jerked when the door opened. She did
not want to turn, and she could feel her heart beating
against her blouse. She was sure it was he, sure because
she felt him, felt the presence of him.

There was a minute of silence before she did look, and
something vaguely like hope collapsed in her. Willie
Kane grinned, and his beady eyes glistened.

"I come for my instruckshuns," he said. The sight of
him was grotesque and horrible and he seemed to enjoy
the expression on Jett's face as she saw him.

"I didn't hire you. Mr. Hetherington hired you. You
can get your orders from him."

"He said the mail was over here and you probably was
too. He said you'd tell me what they was."

"How in hell does *he* know where I am!" Jett pulled
at the envelopes in front of her, looking for the right one,
the one with the truck schedule in it.

Willie Kane giggled. "He knows," he said, but Jett did
not hear him. She found the sheet and read it while he
stood back by the door behind her, and she said, "Crow
Point pickup for this afternoon," without looking at him.

"That all?" The grin was cemented on his twisted face
and she could not bear to look at it there.

"That's all," she said, "and from now on don't come
here! I'll put the information in his box and you get it
from him!"

He giggled again, licking his lips with his tongue and

touching his knotted hand to his forehead, backing out
of the door.

"Just go!" Jett screamed at him, and the door shut,
leaving her alone.

She felt flat and she knew why. She had thought that
Kane would be Hetherington. She thought, Two days
. . . two everlasting days, and then it will be right again.

Instead of putting the mail in Luke's box, she sorted it
and let it stay on the desk. She could not leave him with
such a thorough victory. When he came for it, she would
be abrupt and quick with him. Some semblance of her
superiority would have to emerge in that brief interval,
and then there would be no more anxiety. Vince's books
were stacked along the shelf above the desk and she took
them down to add the new figures and keep the records
up to date. In the midst of her work, she looked at her
watch, and it was past two. He would come soon. She
kept on working.

At three-thirty the sun began to fade, and the spots of
it in the office lessened. Jett had finished with the books
a half hour ago, and she had been sitting there half
waiting, half hoping that he would not come. And he did
not. There was an air of stillness about the building and
Jett felt alone. She got up and looked out at the walk
leading up to the office, but there was no one near. Again
she read her watch. He was probably working with the
yearling, she thought, and she tossed the pencil in her
hand to the desk and walked out of the office.

Jiffy was sitting in the sand outside the barn, and a
groom was washing off a mare near the fence. There was
no one in the paddocks. Jett walked slowly through the
barn and out to the stables.

"Hi, Miss Black!"

Raol was coming from the barrier, still holding the
currying comb he had been using on his pony. "Did you
see the pony my dad got me?"

"No, I didn't. He looks fine." She barely noticed the

horse, but she studied the boy. His resemblance to Luke was strong, and she thought that he was little more than a miniature of Hetherington with a child's disposition.

"My dad had him hauled from Lexington. He's mine!"

Raol smiled proudly, and Jett leaned against the wall watching him. She said, "You're crazy about your dad, aren't you?"

"Sure," Raol answered quickly. "Do you like him?"

"What are you going to call the pony?"

"I don't know yet. I'm going to wait and choose a good name for him. Do you like my dad, Miss Black?"

He was Hetherington's son, all right, Jett thought to herself, with the same cool persistence.

"I haven't thought about it," she said. "Where is he now?"

"He's back by the brood mares with the vet. We're going swimming at five o'clock, up in the quarry. We swim there mornings, but *this* morning the pony came, so we're going tonight instead."

The brood mares were in fall pasture. Luke would be with the veterinarian, and it would provide an ideal time for Jett to come face to face with him. If he attempted to see her alone she would laugh at him. A series of mental images came and went in her brain as she walked down the path. She was becoming obsessed with the contradiction of wanting to see him to prove her independence of him and wanting to avoid him out of fear that she was not impervious to his ways, to the very looks of him. It never occurred to her how he would feel, and it was unimportant.

There was the sound of a banjo strumming lightly from off in the bunkhouse, and a boy was singing.

She felt an irresistible desire to barge into the bunkhouse and demand to know why the boy was not working at a quarter to four in the afternoon. If Blake were at Bel Aire, no one would dare to perform that way in midafternoon. But when she looked up and saw them heading

down the path toward her, she forgot about the boy and
his banjo. Dr. Kaller seemed shrunken beside Luke, and
he took three steps to Luke's one as they walked. Luke
was talking with his eyes straight ahead and he saw Jett,
but there was no change in his expression. The Doctor
beamed and held his hand out to Jett. "Why, Miss Black,
it's been a long time since I've seen you. How's your
daddy?"

Before she could answer, Luke said, "We can take care
of the rest of them tomorrow, Doc," and he waved his
hand behind him as he went on.

"Say," Dr. Kaller said in a confidential tone, "that's
one good man your daddy hired. Why, he knows more
about horses than I do myself, and only this afternoon—"

As he talked, Jett watched the slim, gaunt figure of
Luke Hetherington until it disappeared around the barn.
He had said nothing to her, and his eyes had looked
through her and beyond. She knew then how Luke felt
about her, and about last night. It meant nothing. She
thought that that was the way she had wanted it. It was
the way she wanted it to be, wasn't it? Sure it was. Wasn't
it?

The banjo sounded louder and the singing more rau-
cous. She had not heard a word Dr. Kaller said.

Chapter Twelve

V INCE ordered a Western on white from the pimply-faced cook and sat at the counter of the diner reading the selections on the small jukebox fixed in front of him. He jammed a dime down the mouth of the instrument and listened to the hot jazz blare out. There was no one else in the diner, and it was past two in the afternoon. Blake was next door in the Professional Building, being told the results of the doctor's examinations. Vince already knew them. The doctor had phoned him earlier that day to ask Vince's advice on the best way to make Blake Black understand that the original diagnosis had been thorough and accurate, and that his paralysis was incurable.

"I'm not sure there is a way to make him believe that," Vince had said to the doctor. "He doesn't give up so easily."

The doctor had answered that it was not a case of there being anything to give up, that Blake had surrendered all the life that was in his limbs, and that now it was merely a case of resignation.

"You better tell him that, Doctor," Vince had said. "Just tell him straight."

Blake had agreed to meet Vince after the session. He had left with an air of buoyancy and confidence, insisting on going up in the elevator unassisted, and laughing over his own remark that "it might not be long before I'll be out of this contraption and I'm getting fond of it." Blake was becoming less and less dependent on others to help him with the wheel chair, but Vince knew it was because he believed that it was a temporary crutch. He shuddered when he anticipated Blake's arrival at the diner.

The cook shoved a plate in front of Vince with the

bread sandwich hanging off it. The egg was watery and so was the ketchup, and Vince barely managed to swallow the first bite. He toyed with his coffee and fed the juke-box more coins. It was strange to be in Richmond, away from Bel Aire, and Vince missed the excitement of Jett's presence, the knowledge that she was near. He thought that his musing about Jett, his love of her, was similar to Blake's condition. It was futile and hopeless, but he clung to his own imaginary convictions because there was little else for him to do. He had to believe in something, in someone. Even she lived in a make-believe microcosm, Vince realized, never knowing reality, never once think-ing she would have to know it someday just as everyone does. Maybe she would never have to leave Bel Aire, but she was growing up to become a beautiful woman, sprightly and emotional, and Vince wondered if she would never feel that there was more to life than Blake and the succession of days on the farm. It was useless to speculate. While he lived with them at the farm, Vince became like them. He saw nothing unusual in Jett, and he began to believe as Blake did about the operation and the paralysis—that more could be done. The trip to Rich-mond was good because of that. Vince felt real again, as though he had established or re-established a perspective, and as depressing as it was, it existed.

Blake called to him through the screen door, and Vince hopped off the stool and held the door back while he pulled the chair through the doorway.

"There's a booth in the back," he said, but Blake was already pushing the wheels that way and Vince followed him.

"Hey, mistuh, your sandwich . . ."

"Forget it," Vince said. "Put it on the bill and draw two coffees."

He sat down in the booth while Blake maneuvered the chair into the empty space at the head of it. Blake looked surprisingly calm, but he looked tired too.

"You order coffee, Vince?"

"Coming."

"Well, they can't do anything for me here."

"I'm sorry to hear it," Vince said.

The cook let the coffee cups slide down the counter, and he whistled at Vince, who got up and carried them over to the booth.

"I expected it, you know," Blake said suddenly. "I expected to be told that nothing could be done."

"It was worth a try, anyway," Vince said.

"You're damn right it was! It's worth this try, and the next try, and the try after that. If you want something, you've got to spend time with it," Blake said forcefully. "You've got to believe in it and stay with it. You can have anything if you want it that way, but you've got to want it. I learned not to be a coward, and I'm paying now because I was one. I ran away and got drunk and got hit, and now look at me. But I learned, and that's important."

Three high-school girls came into the diner and sat up on the stools, nudging one another and laughing highly at secret jokes. They tossed a coin to see who would play the jukebox and they played a torch song, with a sirupy-sounding crooner chanting the lyrics.

Blake said, "I don't want this just for myself, Vince. You know that."

"Yes."

"When she was just a kid growing up I used to think of the things we'd do together when she got older—the places we'd go. She had to go to school and all, and I waited some more, but I never stopped thinking that someday I'd take her traveling, let her know something of life besides horses and barn smells and track business."

"You can still do it," Vince said. "Plenty of people see the world, crippled or not." He knew when the words came out that it was the wrong thing to say. Blake set his cup down in the saucer hard.

"I'm not going to stay crippled! Sure, maybe people do

wheel around the world. Don't go by boat or plane—go by wheel chair. Sure! But not me! Not with Jett having to look out for me like a mother hen, worry about me every minute she's with me! What kind of trip would that be for a girl? No, damn it! I'm going to get on my two feet. I've got to!"

The crooner's voice smothered the air, and Vince swallowed the last of the coffee. "Will we start back tonight?"

"Tomorrow night," Blake said. "There's another doctor I want to see before we go. I'll wire Jett we'll be another day."

Luke found the letter in his box. It was on top of the other mail, and it was a blue envelope with black ink scrawling out his name. He set the business correspondence on the ledge in the hallway and ripped the blue envelope open. There was a single sheet of matching stationery, the writing running along the page diagonally. The salutation was absent, and the message did not have a beginning or an ending. It simply read: "I have to see you. To talk with you. Come to the house at four."

He wadded the sheet in a ball and tossed it to the wooden floor. Taking the letters from the ledge, he looked through them, all of them addressed to Blake, most of them from buyers wanting information on the stock, a few from owners anxious to sell their stock. He could tell this by the sender's address, without reading the letters inside. They bulged in his coat pocket when he put them there, and before he left he kicked the wrinkled blue ball of paper on the floor with the toe of his shoe.

It had surprised him. He had not seen her all day, and from her actions the day before, he had guessed that she had reached the same conclusion he had. But now she wanted to see him. Luke pushed the door of the office building open and walked out into the air. It was after three in the afternoon, a gray afternoon with no breeze, and Luke wanted to work an hour with the yearling.

He told himself he did not have time to see her, and he blamed the inclination stirring inside him on curiosity. Yet he could feel the inclination, feel it in the muscles of his legs and in his fingers, and rising in his throat when he thought of her. He did not want to get involved with Jett, not any more than he was, and he vowed he would not, but there was a crazy restlessness in him when he remembered the letter, and he glanced at his watch. It was twenty minutes to four.

He walked straight to the barn and yelled to a swipe to bring the yearling around to the paddock. His thoughts fell over each other seeking answers, but he knew one thing: He would not go to her.

Working with the yearling, he could forget. It was hard work and a good time to do it with the sun behind the clouds. The beast fought, though it knew it would be broken, and Luke liked the fight. A good horse made sure his master *was* a master, and the challenge was honest. It was different with people, Luke knew, because people showed their feelings too soon and changed them too often. That was the reason he would not accept her challenge. Jett was playing—with Luke and with herself—and the game was dangerous then and not sport. When he was finished, he told the swipe to let the yearling run free and he went back to the stable to change his soaking shirt. As he walked inside he felt the coolness on his flesh, and the smell of horses was fine and strong. There was a pipe fixed at the end of the stable, high above, with a spray attachment that took the place of a shower. Luke turned the water on and stripped down. He slipped out of his shoes and stood barefoot on the cement floor under the cold water, letting it run on his back.

Soaping down, he shut his eyes and rubbed his face with the lather. Opening them again, he saw her. Her back was to him, and she was leaning against the stall looking off the other way, but standing there, waiting. With his long arm he reached up and turned the tap off.

He shook his head vigorously and grabbed the old towel '
from the railing, fixing it around his waist.

She did not turn around. "Are you decent?" she said.

"Was I when you came in here?"

"I don't know. I didn't look."

"You just knew it was me, huh?"

She said, "I saw your clothes."

He pulled his pants on his still damp body.

"Well?" she said. "Are you?"

Not waiting for his answer, she turned. The crisp white
dress highlighted the black hair that hung loosely down
to her shoulders, not held back by the ribbon now. On
her feet she wore small ballet slippers that gave her ankles
a thin, graceful line. Her arms and neck were free of
jewelry, and there was a fresh shine to her skin and in
her eyes.

She said, "I know you got my message."

"Yes, I got it." He sat down on the three-legged stool
and put his shoes on, tipped his head and pounded one
side to get the water out of his ear.

"Why didn't you come?"

"I had work," he said, and wondered why he gave her
any excuse at all, why he didn't just tell her that he
wanted no more to do with her. Seeing her smile, seeing
the dress outline her breasts and hips and thighs, he knew
that it was not true; he did want her, a physical want.
That much he wanted to do with her.

"But now you're through work."

Luke discarded the wet shirt he had worked in and
reached to the hook for the dry polo sweater. He pushed
into it and tucked it in at his waist.

He said yes, he was through work.

"And will you come now?"

"Why?"

"I— Don't you *know*?"

"I want to hear you say it," he said, standing up, walking to her. "I want to hear you say it."

"All right. All right, I'll say it. I want to feel you again —feel you touch me. I don't want to think about it. I want to feel it. I've thought about it until I'm sick with it. I want to be able to sleep again, the way I slept that night after you left—the way I haven't slept since then. Listen, I—"

Luke grabbed her arms and kissed her hard. He pushed her backward until she was inside the small stall, and then when he touched her shoulders she seemed to sink backward, falling to the hay.

She whispered, "Luke! Luke!"

His hands found the buttons of her dress, slipped them open, and touched the bare skin at her waist. He looked at her eyes and they were closed. The sigh from her made her whole body tremble.

He heard her say, "Please, oh, please!" and he forced her mouth shut with his lips. . . .

Afterward she said nothing and Luke held her hand in his. The stable was quiet, and Luke could not stop thanking God that no one had interrupted them. It had been a chance, a magnificent impulse that swept them both, and it had been great and perfect with no one and nothing to interfere. Not even thinking had interfered, Luke realized, or pride, or fear, and it was good.

"Luke?"

"Yes?"

"This was the first time, wasn't it? Wasn't this the first time for us?"

He said, "Yes, this was the first time."

He turned to her and took her in his arms, his palms pressing against her shoulders and the arch of her back. The moistness on her cheeks startled him and he held her away from himself and saw her crying. With his fingers he touched the tears as though they were strange and curious, and her body convulsed with sobbing as she bolted forward and clung hard to him.

"Will you help me, Luke?" she asked. "Will you?"

Chapter Thirteen

"YOU DO UNDERSTAND, don't you?"

She lay on her back, the clay ground under her, the azure sky above with the green patches of tall tree branches swaying lazily in the gentle wind. Her shirt, open at the neck, was the color of the bark on the trees, a rich dark brown, and her jodhpurs matched the dusty gray color of the trail they had come over to this spot. Luke lay beside her, his big hands and arms behind his head, his eyes shut, listening to her talk. He wore the same faded jeans with the soiled polo shirt and the round skullcap covering his short-cropped light hair. A few yards away the two horses, tied to the trees, poked their long noses down into the grass and swallowed it up into their mouths, snorting and tapping their hind feet nervously.

"But what makes you think he's going to get well?" Luke said.

"You don't know Blake."

"Well, what is it? Haven't you ever had dates? I mean, he's seen you with men before, hasn't he?"

Jett sat up and ran her fingers through her long black hair. She looked down at Luke and suddenly she wanted to tell him. But she was not sure herself what there was to say. She felt the guilt, magnified when she thought of Blake, and being with Luke that way, trying to explain half-truths, Jett felt ashamed.

She said, "You don't understand yet, do you? You see, I'm all that Blake has. It would kill him."

"Just to see us together? What the hell!"

"Look, Luke! I know Blake! I know what will hurt him and what won't! Will you do it my way? For now, do it my way!"

Luke laughed. He reached up for her and brought her

97

down on his chest. Their kiss began playfully and mounted until it was intense and hard. They came apart and Jett let her head rest in the hollow of Luke's neck, waiting for her own breathing to be slower. With his fingers Luke touched her hair, pulling it away from her ears and smoothing it back.

"When will he be back?" he said.

"Tonight, probably. Around dinnertime."

She shut her eyes and tried not to think about Blake's return, but her mind would not stray away from the inevitable. With Luke she had the memory of a sudden new love, a physical emotion that tore through her body and ate at her emotions and made her want him. A three-day-old child of her passions. Yet there were years of Blake, long years that Jett cherished and could not be without. In time, in the space of several hours, she would have to deal with both, and she would not let herself believe that it would be a match to see which was the strongest. They were both strong, and she needed their strength. One would not defeat the other, she thought, so long as neither was aware of his opponent.

"Luke," she said, "you will try to understand, won't you? I don't want to be responsible again for Blake's being hurt."

"Again?"

"I mean I don't want him to be hurt again."

"O.K. for now. Have it your way for now. But remember something, Jett. I'm not very sympathetic with this business of pretending things aren't the way they are just to save someone's feelings. It's foolish, and it usually works out—"

"But you will. You will be careful?"

"Yeah, I'll try."

Luke looked at the watch strapped to his wrist and whistled. "Eleven-thirty! We've been out here all morning! There's a fellow coming from Waynesboro at twelve to see the yearling!"

They got up and Jett brushed the dust from her pants. She looked up at Luke once more, and her hands touched his waist, her thumbs sliding down under the belt on his jeans. Her body snapped and pressed hard against his as he leaned down and gave her his mouth. Minutes later they walked quietly to the horses, mounted, and rode back fast.

Vince helped Blake get into the wheel chair on the drive where the car was stopped. Bel Aire seemed quiet and there was an air of lethargy encompassing the grounds, except for the impatient figure of a short, fat man pacing back and forth on the walk in front of the office.

"I'll see who he is," Blake said. "Get the bags out and put the car up for the day. I don't see a damn soul here."

"We're early."

"That doesn't mean the place should be deserted!"

"Probably down by the paddocks," Vince answered, pulling his suit coat off and tossing it in the front seat of the car. He crawled in and started the motor and Blake pushed the wheels of his chair vigorously, heading off toward the office. Vince pitied him, pitied the way Blake hung on to that thread of hope, knowing all too well that it would not hold him, that it would break and send him spiraling down to firm ground and fact. The second doctor Blake had seen in Richmond had reiterated what Sellers first told Blake, and Blake, no less hopeful, no less convinced that those men were fools, had told Vince as they were driving back that he was going to New York soon to see another specialist. Vince cut the motor inside the garage and started hauling the baggage out of the back.

The little man had a cigar in his right hand, and he held his little finger up as he smoked, the diamond ring he wore there catching the sun's rays and forcing Blake to squint as he approached.

"Hello there!" Blake called out, and the man turned and looked at him.

He waited until Blake was in front of him, and then he said, "You Mr. Hetherington?"

"No, I'm Blake Black. Can I help you?"

"On the phone I talked to a Mr. Hetherington. Where's he at?"

"I don't know, offhand. Maybe down by the paddocks."

"I been down there," the man said in an irritated tone. "They didn't know where he was, either. Said he'd meet me here at twelve and he's not here. What kind of business is he running?"

Blake shifted his body in the chair and looked up at the man. "Bel Aire's my farm," he told him. "I run it. Hetherington works for me."

"Don't matter. I talked to Hetherington. Like to do business with the man I talked to in the first place."

He spat a sliver of the cigar from his mouth and puffed another cloud out into the air. Blake studied him for a moment, and then, pushing the wheels of his chair, he said, "Follow me into the office. I'll get hold of Hetherington and you can talk with him there."

The man waddled behind Blake, throwing the cigar over his shoulder and hawking and coughing while he held a handkerchief to his nose and blew into it as he went. Inside he explained that he had come to see a yearling he called about a day ago, and he drove all the way from Waynesboro.

"I try to be on time," he said, "and then *this* happens!"

Blake grabbed the phone on his desk and buzzed the stable. A swipe told him he saw Luke Hetherington at breakfast but not after, and to try the barn. At the barn, a hand said he had not seen Hetherington since yesterday. The heat was penetrating Blake's suit and shirt and he felt sopping wet from the sweat on his body. He loosened his tie and pushed the button to the mess shed. Before the answer came, he saw them.

The horses stopped a few feet away from the office, and Blake watched Luke swing his right leg over the animal's back and slip his left foot out of the stirrup. They were both laughing. Jett's face was flushed with color and her head was thrown back as she laughed, her eyes wide and shining. Blake let the neck of the phone fall in its cradle.

"Maybe he just don't want to do business," the fat man said then.

"Shut up!" Blake finally shouted. "Shut up! He's coming in now, for God's sake!"

The fat man said nothing. He seemed to lose some of his belligerence, and as Blake wheeled past him the man lowered his eyes and coughed self-consciously.

The door of the office slammed behind Blake, and he maneuvered himself down the hall. The door at the end opened suddenly and Hetherington strode forward rapidly, colliding with Blake.

"Where the hell have you been?" Blake demanded. "Man in there waiting for you. Said he had an appointment with you."

"I'm ten minutes late, that's all."

"You don't *have* to be one minute late if you know what you're doing. Where you been?"

"I'm getting later all the time I stand here talking," Luke answered. He did not wait for Blake to shout at him again, but went on down the hall to the office. Blake heard him open the door and greet the man, and he heard the man laugh at something Luke had said. He took the wheel chair the rest of the way down the hallway and out onto the steps, where he saw Jett perched on her horse's back, holding the reins of the horse Luke had been riding. She looked beautiful and poised, and her face was relaxed in a way that Blake loved and had missed seeing since his accident. There was no concern in her eyes now, and no slight frown on her forehead. Her lips were parted, and her eyes looked out at the stables and then up to the house and finally to the steps of the office. At first

she stared at him as though he were not there, and then,
leaning forward in her saddle, she believed what she saw.
She cried out his name, and pulling herself from the
horse's back, she dropped both pairs of reins and ran
forward to him, shouting his name now.

Her arms went about his shoulders, hugging him
fiercely, and her dark eyes filled with quick tears. Kissing
his cheeks and holding his hand, she said, "You're back,
Bunny!" and the tone of her words was incredulous,
almost as though she had not really believed that he was
coming back at all.

She knelt beside him there on the steps, and Blake took
his handkerchief from his pocket and handed it to her.
As she touched it to her eyes, Luke Hetherington came
through the doorway of the building with the fat man at
his heels. Luke looked down at her, at the handkerchief
in her hand and the tears on her cheeks. He paused longer
than was necessary to pass Blake and Jett, and the fat
man bit off the end of another cigar and scratched the
brick with a match. Then Luke looked ahead of him and
said, "It's over this way," and the pair walked off the
steps and down the slate path toward the paddocks.

"Want to go inside?" Blake said, and Jett nodded. As
she walked behind Blake she felt a bitter resentment at
the way Luke had lingered as he passed and watched her.
The resentment was tinged with fear, and Jett wondered
if she was frightened of Luke's ability to see through
relationships, to go beyond the surface and reach the core.

Once that morning he had said, "You always speak as
though you were doing your dad a favor and you weren't
gaining anything yourself. It's a fishy setup, Jett, but if
you say so, who am I?"

That happened after she had tried to explain that they
—she and Luke—must never let Blake know that they had
even *talked* intimately. She had said to Luke, "It's hard
on me. Don't you realize that I'm going to suffer plenty?
But I can't let Blake down. He needs me so."

On the steps, kneeling at Blake's feet, weeping over his return, Jett knew that it had looked the other way around. Luke's long glance seemed to express surprise, and at the same time, that kind of surprise that one half anticipates, as though Luke himself had expected to discover Jett reacting that way to her father's return.

Jett sat in the chair at the side of Blake's desk. He loosened the collar of his shirt and untied the navy-blue tie, placing it on his lap. Folding his arms, he looked at her and smiled.

"It's good to be back," he said simply.

"Bunny, did they—"

"No, nothing. It'll take time, Cricket. Time."

"But did the doctor say that there was a chance?"

A nerve in Blake's forehead pulsed, and he looked away from her, out the window, where he saw a boy leading the horses away. He remembered the way he had seen Jett and Luke ride up, the way Jett had looked. Instantly he wanted to stop talking about doctors and his condition and ask her point-blank where she had been with Luke Hetherington and how well she knew him. He did not believe that Jett was even mildly interested in Hetherington, but he needed her assurance, needed to be told that by her. Still, he despised himself for that necessity, detested the raw jealousy rising up in him. He had no way of justifying his desire for his daughter, his unwillingness to share his possession with another, and yet his lack of justification did not temper the feeling that Jett was his uniquely. Turning his eyes on her, he saw the perfect beauty of her face and of her whole body, and remembering that night months ago when he held her in the early morning, he wished now that he had been more a man and less a father. In his present situation, he could not be a man, and the teasing suggestion that he might one day defy convention was crippled in the same way he was. But when he was well again? Blake clenched his fist and shook his head.

"What is it, Bunny? Did they say there wasn't?"

"Wasn't what?"

"A chance!"

"No, of course they didn't say that!"

She sat back, alarmed at the anger in his voice. He grinned sheepishly and told her that he was tired from his trip, asking her to forgive him for being so blunt. Blake looked older then, and for the first time Jett felt more than sympathy with him. She felt plain pity, and she never had before. Not for anyone, and certainly never for Blake. The emotion depressed her, sickened her thoughts. She was glad when he said, "Let's talk about something else. If you reach in my pocket here, I think you'll find a small box."

Jett winked at Blake and leaned over to fish the box from the pocket of his dark suit. "You always remember me," she said, snapping the string and lifting the cardboard top. There was a thin golden bracelet lying on the soft piece of cotton inside, and Jett raised it in the air and let it hang in the light. "Beautiful, Bunny! It's simply beautiful!"

She fastened it to her wrist and turned it at odd angles to admire it. The frown vanished from her face and the lines on her forehead diminished. When she looked up at Blake, he knew that in that instant she was her old self again, and he was what he had always been for her. He could not resist fortifying himself further.

"Tell me," he said, "what you've been doing since Vince and I've been away."

"I guess I told you over the phone that Bella Donna took well."

"Good. Did you help Hetherington with it?"

"Yes. There really wasn't much to do. It was a natural."

"And Kaller came, I suppose, to check the brood mares."

"Two days ago."

Blake reached for a cigarette and Jett took the small

carton of matches from the desk and lighted it for him.

"And tell me," Blake said, letting the smoke play out in the air, "how about Hetherington? You two seem to be getting along better."

"Not really."

"No? I thought you were."

"I merely helped him with the work. The way you wanted."

"Didn't you ride together this morning?"

He tried to make the question sound unimportant, but the words seemed to accuse her. Jett caught the accusation in his tone. She answered, "Look, Bunny, you certainly don't think just because I ride with someone that means we're hitting it off in great style. No! I met him on the trail and rode back here with him."

"Don't get excited, Cricket. I'd be happy if you and Hetherington did get along better. I'd hoped you'd get to know each other while I was away."

"Well, it didn't happen that way!" Jett told him. She stood up and went to the window. "Vince is coming with the baggage," she said. "We going up to the house for some lunch?"

"I'll be along in a while, honey. I want to check over things here. You can go on and get things started. Vince will help get the suitcases up when I'm ready to go."

She walked over to him and put her hands on his shoulders, standing behind him as he sat in the wheel chair. Her fingers smoothed the black strand of hair back from his forehead, and she bent down to put her lips on his neck. "Bunny, thanks for the bracelet."

"I'm glad you like it," Blake answered. His confidence was restored then, after listening to Jett speak of Hetherington, and feeling her touch, he blamed himself for being a brooding crank—the mark of an invalid. Blake vowed he would not let himself conjure up any further doubts. He would be secure in his love of Jett as he always had been before the accident. Secretly he laughed when he thought of Hetherington threatening his security. The next thing he knew, he thought, he would be suspecting Vince of intruding there.

"Don't stay too long, Bunny," Jett said. "I'll be waiting for you."

In the sunlight as she walked from the office, the bracelet sparkled with rich color. She drew a deep breath and was thankful for the fresh air and the green grass she walked over. It was still like summer there at Bel Aire in mid-October. The sky was a summer sky, almost pure blue with only a faint trace of white cloud threads, and the breeze was lazy. She wished only to think of the day, the way it looked and felt on her skin as she walked in it, but the incidents of the day boomeranged each time she threw them off and tried to alienate them. With amazement she realized that she had lied to both Luke and Blake, and that she did not even know the truth herself. Her guilt was parallel, and yet not truly parallel, because at several points the sides touched and became one. Blake was her father and she must not let him be hurt. Luke was her lover and she would not let that love be hurt. That was simple, but it was not true. Because there was more to her and Blake, much more, and if he did get well, she thought, if he did, then she would not need Luke. And even that was false, that thought, like all the rest. There were no more truths. There were only minutes, and lies, and a confusion like a massive cobweb that weaved in and out, delicate and fragile, but sturdy for those it served.

As she passed the field at the foot of the hill, Jett saw the twisted form leaning passively on the ground against the fence. Willie Kane's eyes were shut and his contorted face was turned to the sun. She walked closer to him and stared down at his ugliness. Somehow his bizarre look symbolized all she had known these last few days, perhaps all she had ever known, and she found it impossible to believe that this glob of flesh lived and felt and was alive.

With the toe of her boot she kicked him hard, reaching his chest, and bringing her foot back again to repeat the blow. He jumped and opened his eyes, staring up at her, his mouth spreading and falling to one side.

"I ain't doing nothing," he said, backing up against the fence.

"That's just the trouble! Get up!"

Slowly, fearfully, Willie raised himself, never taking his eyes from her. His back rubbed the fence, and his mouth became wider as he emitted a cackling sound, hoarse and high-pitched.

"You better leave me alone. You better or you'll be sorry!"

Jett hated the sight of him. She felt a compulsion to crack him across the face and she moved toward him, watching his yellow eyes dart from hers to the field beyond the fence. Before she could reach him, he hobbled back, flung himself over the fence like an animal being chased, and ran a few feet on the other side before he stopped. He turned and looked back at her, shaking his fist in an obscene way at first, and then laughing, shrilly and hysterically, as she turned and hurried up the hill away from him.

Chapter Fourteen

A WEEK LATER the fat man came back to pick up the yearling. Luke and Vince were hauling the horse into the trailer at the rear of the large red Packard convertible while the man stood sucking on his wet cigar and watching.

"I shoulda recognized him, I guess, but goddamned if I did," he said to Luke. "How long he been that way?"

"I don't know. A few months."

"Three," Vince said.

"Course, I never met him, personally, that is, but I heard of him, all right. Hell, darn near everyone heard of Blake Black."

Once the yearling was inside, Luke snapped the wooden door shut and heard the scared whinny of the beast. "All ready now," he said.

"Don't he have a daughter?" The man flicked a long ash from the cigar and stuck a pudgy hand in his coat pocket, pulling the sides of the jacket apart to expose his round, protruding stomach under the sweat-stained bright orange shirt he wore.

Vince answered him. "Yes, he does."

"I think I saw her that last day I was here. Didn't I see her? She was standing on the steps—kneeling she was—and she was crying. That her I saw?"

He looked directly at Luke, anticipating some comment from him, but Luke merely nodded, and the fat man said, "She was right pretty. Looked just like him, too, in a way."

Vince took the green bills the man pulled from his pocket and counted them silently. Luke was still, remembering the picture of Jett and her father that the man's words called up. He himself had not seen Jett since that moment a week ago. He had not even heard from her or about her. Those first few days away from her, he had imagined many things. Perhaps Blake had found out about them and forbidden her to see him. She may have changed her mind since Blake came home. Illness, maybe. Anything could have caused her absence, and Luke was hot with curiosity. Once, that Tuesday evening on the third day, after Raol had gone to sleep and the swipes and other workers had started their evening crap game, Luke had gone halfway up the hill, wanting to knock on the door of the house on some pretense to see if she were all right. Then he remembered that he had promised her he would not give her father any reason to believe there might be something between them, and his very presence, despite a pretense of some kind, might feed any suspicion Blake had. Luke had retraced his steps and walked back to the cabin to face another sleepless night.

As the days passed, the fifth, the sixth, and now the seventh, he forced her image from his thoughts, threw himself into the work at Bel Aire, and tried to let time answer his questions about her. The fat man had renewed all of Luke's wonder and fear in that brief interval when he spoke of her. Vince rarely mentioned her, and that week he had not said anything about her, Blake, or the trip. Luke did not understand why he felt a bond with Vince, as though they both agreed on something without needing to explain whatever it was to the other.

"Well, it's a pleasure," the man said, sticking his thick, short fingers out to shake hands with them. " 'Spect I'll be around to see you all again someday."

He opened the door of the Packard and climbed into the front seat. The cigar was barely an inch long, but still wet and half smoky in his mouth, clenched sloppily between his huge white teeth. He grinned at them and the roar of the motor drowned out his good-by. Luke and Vince turned to walk away.

"See Boris is sick?" Vince said.

"Bad leg. I rode him the other afternoon and he went crazy on me for a second. Stumbled and sprained it, I guess."

Vince pursed his lips and whistled tonelessly as they walked along. Instead of working up to fall days, the weather seemed to be going backward, back to the kind of heat expected in August. The sun bore down on them, and that day the breeze was far away. Luke's thoughts shifted to Raol, who was at the quarry with Jiffy.

He said, "I'm thinking of sending the boy to school in Hillsboro. Let him go afternoons."

Vince nodded and said he thought it was a good idea. When they came to the split in the path from the office to the stable, Vince announced that Blake and he were going over the September accounts.

"You want to sit in? No need to, really, but if you're curious . . ."

"No, thanks," Luke said. "I think I understand them. I looked through some of it while you were gone."

They went in opposite directions, and Luke stopped by the gate to the paddock and took his tobacco pouch from his jeans pocket. He loaded his pipe and sat smoking, his weight thrown against the white railing. As if to torture himself, he made himself remember the intricate details of his hours with Jett, gesture for gesture, word for word. His memory was too perfect, and it wrecked what strength he had to keep him from going to her. Blake was at the office with Vince, and Luke knew that he had a clear afternoon, with nothing pressing to be done and no commitments. A week was too long.

She answered the door. The flowered silk skirt clung to her hips and thighs, and the black blouse was cut simply, round at the neck and where her breasts were. She wore rope sandals that tied about her slim ankles and made her bare legs seem longer, and on her wrist a gold bracelet was fastened loosely.

He stepped in and she did not stop him. The kitchen

had the good smell of a roast cooking in the oven, and
there was a cookbook tilted up against some red jars on
the table near the window.

"I had to come here."

"I know."

They stood in the center of the kitchen facing each
other.

"What was the matter?"

She looked at him and did not answer. The clock fixed
on the wall ticked loudly. Her eyes fell to the floor.

"Tell me!" Luke said.

"I can't."

She would not look at him. Luke took a step forward
and she backed away.

"Don't come closer."

"Jett, what's the matter with you?" He took her wrists
in his hand and held them tight. She struggled to be free,
and the bracelet cut into her flesh. Her eyes met his and
she stopped moving.

"Luke?"

"What?"

"I don't know what to do." He felt her body against
his and her arms at his shoulders. Her lips were wet on
his chest where his shirt opened, and she kept saying she
didn't know what to do.

"I couldn't stand it," she said, "being away from you.
You don't know what it's been like, Luke. Making cakes
and pies and cooking, trying to keep busy, trying to stay
away from down there, giving up the horses even, the
rides that would make me feel better, so I wouldn't see
you. It's been like a tightrope and one false move and
I'd fall, and all the time Blake's been here, watching,
watching to see if I was going to fall."

"He knows?"

"No. That's just it. He doesn't know. He keeps asking
me why I want to stay here. Why I don't want to ride.
Then I read into what he says and I get afraid he knows.

He asked, you know. He asked how we were getting along and I thought he knew then, and I tried to cover up—"

"For the love of Mike!" Luke interrupted her harshly. "You're making too much out of this. You're old enough, for God's sake. You're not a little kid. Tell him! Tell him!"

"I can't!" she said. "Luke, I can't tell Blake." She began to cry. Luke lifted her up and carried her down the hall into the wide living room, where the sun was streaming in through the windows. He put her on the couch and let her cry, and he did not know what she could be thinking, what could be stabbing at her that way.

If he had come to the house the night Blake returned he might have prevented it. For Blake was exhausted from the trip, and from his reorientation to the work at Bel Aire, and the dinner had stuffed him, making him weary. Jett thought of it as she buried her head in Luke's lap.

"Bunny, can I bring you anything?" She had sat on the bed beside him.

"Just talk for a while before I put the light out and call it a night." He had learned to dress and undress himself. The green cotton pajamas under his light robe were new, and Jett remarked that she liked the color. "They make you look gay," she said, "and you should be. I'm afraid you worry too much, Blake."

"You're my only real worry."

"Me?"

"Yes," he said. "I worry about you—and the future."

"That's silly, Bunny."

"Is it? Jett, you're all I have. All I've ever had, really. The farm, the money, this house—they wouldn't have any meaning without you."

"I'm not going away, Blake. Not now—not ever."

"I tried to send you away once, Jett, remember? No, don't stop me. I want to talk about it. I tried to send you away because I was a coward. You said I didn't talk about things. I ran away from them or pretended they never happened. Cricket, you were right. I've been thinking about it. A man thinks more when he's strapped down the way I've been. . . . What I'm trying to tell you is that I don't have that shame any more—that guilt, if you want to use that word. About us, I mean. Maybe we're different from other fathers and daughters, and maybe we're not. I don't know, and I don't care. I only know that I love you, Jett, and I only care about having you with me. Always having you with me."

He took her hand then and his grip was powerful. What he had said, and the way he pressed against her, forced Jett to pull away suddenly, to wrench herself free from him. She leaped to her feet, startled, looking down at him, while he stared back, shock keen in his eyes.

"Jett!"

At the sound of his voice, half alarmed, half commanding, she fell onto the bed beside him, clinging to him, unable to cry, her teeth clenched together tightly, her lips trembling. His arms seemed to envelop her, and she could hear him comfort her, his voice husky with emotion.

"I know, Jett. I know how you feel. But I'll get well. I will, Cricket. You believe that, don't you?"

The pity swelled inside her, sheer pity, and disgust at herself for what she was thinking. She was remembering Luke's arms around her body, remembering and daring to compare, knowing that there was no comparison.

She could not remember how long she lay beside him, listening to him talk that way.

The sobbing stopped abruptly. Luke reached down and raised her chin, turning her face to his. After all that, her beauty was still unchanged, her eyes wet, but not red and puffed, the soft skin on her cheeks radiant despite the moist streaks left there from her tears. Luke realized that he meant what he was going to say. He meant it, not only because she was so lovely to see, but because his whole self was saturated with her, everything about her, even the cryptic sides of her that he did not yet understand.

"I love you, Jett," he said. His voice showed none of the ripe emotion he felt singing through him, nor did he inflect his words in any way to make them more attractive, more penetrating. It was a statement of fact, and it had been spoken simply, clearly. Jett let him take her to him, allowing herself to have him there because it was right and real and the only thing she wanted then more than anything or anyone else.

The wheels of Blake's chair caught on the stone midway up the hill. He swore, and Vince was annoyed with his mounting impatience.

"I don't know why you think he'd be at the house."

Blake snarled. "I don't know why he'd be there either, but he's not anyplace else. The horses are all in. He didn't just vanish into space, for God's sake."

"He's probably at the quarry or in the woods."

"His son just got back from there. He said he wasn't around. Hetherington's got a habit of being unavailable when he's wanted, and I'm sick of it!"

Vince sighed and pushed the chair strenuously up the path to the house. "We don't really need him, anyway, Blake. I can tell him about the account when I see him. It isn't a matter of life and death."

"What the hell are you taking up for him for? He works for me and I've got a right to be curious about what he does on my time!"

As they reached the top of the hill, a scant breeze hit Vince's face and relieved the feel of the sweat pouring over him. He paused on the level ground and wiped his forehead. Blake spun the wheels with his hand and went ahead.

"Do you want me to come along?"

Blake said, "You're damn right!"

Following behind him, Vince swallowed a mean oath. Blake was becoming desperately demanding lately, and he was queerly perverse about Luke Hetherington. In the beginning, he had accepted Hetherington, accepted him and praised him. Now he was dissatisfied, wrongly so, Vince felt, because Luke was more than adequate in the job. He did more than his share of work at the farm, too, faster than most men could have accomplished the same tasks.

The trip to Richmond had soured him. Vince could not blame him for that.

At the door, before Vince could work the chair up the steps, Blake thundered out her name. "Jett! Jett!"

From the back of the house they heard her answer, and when Vince eased the chair into the kitchen, Jett came down the hall, her slim body covered by a mint-green wrapper tied at her waist, her long black hair combed loosely.

"What's the matter, Blake?"

"Is Hetherington here?"

"Hetherington!" She tried to keep her voice steady.

"He's noplace around," Blake said. "I thought he might be here."

"This is the last place he'd be, and you know it!" Jett's voice was sharp with the right amount of indignation, and Blake looked away. "I guess I just got foggy for a while or something," he said. He leaned back in the wheel chair, his hands fidgeting, a look of regret on his face, regret for the way he had come there to accuse her. He bit his lip and began to dig in his pockets for a cigarette.

"How many has he had today?" Jett asked Vince. "He's not supposed to smoke so much."

Trying to smile, Blake shoved the pack back into his pocket. He sat there helplessly, like an actor who had come on stage at the wrong time, unable to think of any lines that would excuse his presence.

"I guess maybe Hetherington went into town or something," Blake said. "We can tell him about the accounts tomorrow."

Vince knew then why Blake had insisted on rushing to the house in the midst of their business, at the moment he had discovered Hetherington's absence around the grounds. Blake was suspicious of Luke, afraid he and Jett were seeing each other surreptitiously. Shuffling his feet nervously, Vince was aware of the tense atmosphere between father and daughter, and he wondered how much of this twisted thinking Jett was subjected to now that Blake's bitterness was coming to the surface. She was bearing up well under the strain. He admired the way she tried to change the subject and make all three more comfortable in that moment.   .

At the oven, Jett opened the door and poked the roast with a knife.

"Pork roast," she said, smiling at Blake. "Your favorite."

She could feel her heart hammer against her skin. If Blake had come a half hour sooner, she thought . . . God, if Blake had arrived here just thirty minutes sooner!

"Well," Blake's words interrupted her thinking, "I guess Vince and I can finish our business in the front room."

"I'll make some iced tea for you," Jett said.

"You go ahead, Vince, and I'll help Cricket for a moment."

Blake was silent until Vince's steps sounded farther away. He watched Jett reach for the tea jar on the shelf, take the cups from their hooks, and stack the three saucers beside them. She could feel him watching her, and his eyes made her self-conscious and ridiculously fearful that he might be able to tell. He might be able to tell by looking at her that an hour ago Luke and she had . . .

"Cricket?"

"Yes, Blake?"

"I didn't mean to sound cranky when I came in a while ago. I know I was impatient and everything, and I guess I took it out on you."

"I didn't mind *that* so much. It was just the idea of that man being *here*. Bunny, what would he come here for?"

"I wasn't being logical, Jett. I couldn't find him, and I decided to look. No sense to it at all."

She let the water boil on the stove and turned to face Blake. She grinned and winked at him. "Forget it," she said. "Blame it on this Indian summer we're all going through."

He came closer to her, spinning the wheels of his chair as he moved. As if to console him, Jett put her fingers out and touched his black hair, smoothing it down and admiring the thickness of it. It was then that she remembered.

At the square window in the living room, Vince looked out at the sunset, purple and pink and blue in the sky beyond the glass. A thought that had been recurrent through the past few days returned, and he examined it momentarily. There were other farms, he knew, and other jobs. He was still young, and at Bel Aire he was static. Static and stagnant, perhaps staying only because it was so unreal. Jett too—he would not pretend otherwise to himself—was a major reason for his desire to stay there.

He turned when he heard her voice in the hall.

"I'll be back in a second, Bunny. I left something in the living room."

She came to a sudden halt in the doorway. Her eyes darted around the room and Vince followed her glance until it came to rest at a portion of the rug under the couch. The soiled cap lay there conspicuously. No one on the farm could mistake the cap's owner. It was a trade-mark, the most noticeable possession Luke Hether-

ington had. In the first second when both of their eyes
fixed on the round felt object, the cracking sound of
Blake's wheel chair could be heard following after Jett,
coming down the hallway. She looked up quickly, a sense
of horror in her black eyes, horror and fear, and Vince
felt as though a bolt of electricity had suddenly charged
the air. The meaning of the cap, the explanation of
Luke's absence, the small drama Jett had played so con-
vincingly became significant and overwhelmingly surprising in that instant. Vince crossed the room suddenly
and picked up the cap, holding it out to Jett. She could
not take it before Blake reached the entrance to the
living room, and Vince crammed it into the pocket of his
trousers a half second before Blake's wheel chair came in
sight.

"I could have got what you wanted in here for you,
Jett. What was it?"

Jett could not answer him. Her eyes raced frantically
from object to object, her mind searching feverishly for
something to pick up. Vince saw the red tray on the cedar
shelf over the fireplace.

"I'll reach it for you," he said, walking over to it, pulling it down.

She turned and faced him. Her look met his squarely
and with a keen directness: "Yes," she said slowly. "Thank
you, Vince. I thought we ought to make a party out of
this. We've never even used the tray, and after all, this
is an occasion."

Vince handed it to her and looked away at Blake.
Blake's face broke into a smile. "I vote we hold all our
meetings up here," he said. "How about that, Vince?
Look at the service we get!"

He laughed then, patting Jett's waist playfully as she
passed in front of him to take the tray to the kitchen.

Chapter Fifteen

I T WAS EARLY the next morning when Jett rode to the quarry. She tied her horse to a tree and walked to the edge of the bank. The stones glowed in the sun's rays, and the ring of blue water was motionless except for a spot in the middle where Raol splashed and kicked as he swam across to meet her. Jett sat on the damp earth and pulled a pair of lightweight gray slacks from her legs. She folded them and set them under the tree she leaned against. She unbuttoned her navy blouse and slipped it off, exposing gleaming white shoulders and a brief but full halter that matched the short white pants of her swim suit. She watched Raol's figure come closer and sat hugging her knees, letting the cool air chill her slightly under the shade of the tree's large branches.

No one but Luke and Raol ever used the quarry for swimming. It was a long way through the woods from Bel Aire, and the location had remained strangely foreign to the workers, and to Jett and Blake as well. There was good swimming at a lake about a mile from the farm, and those who did swim preferred to go the longer distance. The quarry was believed to be bottomless, and to reach the water it was necessary to dive from the bank circling it. The bank itself was rough and rocky in contrast to the sand beach of the lake. Jett had decided last night that it was the perfect place to meet Luke and talk with him. She had left the house at seven, knowing Blake would sleep until ten, and she had fully expected to find Luke there swimming with Raol. She imagined that he would come there soon, that perhaps he was already on his way, for he had told her that it was a regular morning ritual for him and his son.

Jett *had* to talk with him. After her experience yesterday she was determined not to risk being caught by Blake again. Vince knew now, she was sure, but she was sure too that Vince would never tell Blake, never indicate that he knew anything about Jett and Luke. She did not know why she trusted Vince so completely, but instinctively she did, perhaps unwisely, she thought to herself. He might be just the one to add season to Blake's growing doubts, and he might have planted the suspicions already blossoming in Blake's mind. Jett rejected the idea immediately, but retained the germ of possibility. Anything was possible, and the tightrope she walked seemed more and more wavering and unsteady. She had decided what she must do, and she had only to convince Luke that it was necessary and important.

There was no question in her mind that she loved Luke, loved him too well to lose him now. The obsession she had known for Blake had gradually diminished and evolved into a status of mixed love and pity. As a man— as a man who was once strong enough to be idolized and adamant enough to hold his idol away from him because of his own inner convictions—she pitied him. He had changed, grown weaker and more dependent, not merely in the physical sense, but morally and spiritually weaker. She had seen him beg, promise, apologize, and hope aloud, the way a weak man does, only half believing his own words. If it had not been for Luke, Jett thought that she might not have seen the change in Blake, that she might have accepted it and become bogged down in a mire of false and dangerous emotion. Luke had shown her love between man and woman, and as a result, she knew for the first time what love between father and daughter was. The words came on her lips: "Father . . . Dad . . ." She tested them loud softly to hear their sound in her voice. It was not yet quite real to her, but it was promising, and Luke would help her fulfill the promise just as he had motivated it.

Raol scrambled up the steep side of the quarry bank

and stood before Jett, his skimpy green trunks dripping, his thin shoulders and arms shivering.

"Hi there," he said. " 'S warmer in the water."

Jett reached for her towel and tossed it to him. He huddled under it, moving back a few feet so that the sun could warm him.

"Going swimming?" he asked.

"I hope so—soon. . . . Is your dad coming out?"

Raol's teeth chattered and he rubbed the towel over his body vigorously.

"He oughta. I came out ahead of him 'cause he was busy when I wanted to leave. Thought he'd be here by now. When I saw you I thought he was with you."

"I'll wait for him, I guess," Jett said, "before I brave the water."

Raol walked over to a tree several yards away and reached for a pair of faded overalls. He picked up a sweat shirt lying beside the pants and chucked two sneakers under his arm. Coming back over to Jett, he said, "Didn't mean to use your towel. I never use one much, but I didn't think when you threw it to me and it's so c-c-cold!"

She assured him that it was all right and watched him pull the overalls over his wet suit. He slipped his hands into the sleeves of the sweater and pulled it down over his head, tucking it in at the waist.

"I'm not going to wait for him, Miss Black. Me and Jiffy are hunting field mice. Find 'em under rocks out in the fields, and me and Jiffy are going to get a batch of 'em after breakfast."

Jett smiled at the boy. "What are field mice good for, Raol?"

"For training. Me and Jiffy will teach 'em to do things. Like a circus, y'know. It won't take long, either." He sat down and shoved his small feet into the sneakers. "You know my dad may send me off to school in town?"

"I didn't know that."

"I don't like it, Miss Black," he said seriously "Going to school's for sissies Jiffy don't have to go He says no one he knows goes to school!"

"I went, Raol I liked it " Jett was surprised at the calm way she had lied, and at the way she was talking to Luke's child, easy and friendly She had never cared much for children in the past, but now she found that she enjoyed them At least, she enjoyed Raol He was so much like Luke, independent and opinionated even at six

"My mother never went and she was smart She could sing like a hummingbird, and she was pretty too "

"You miss her very much, don't you?"

Raol shrugged his shoulders and stood up, looking down at Jett "I guess," he said, "I didn't really know her well   Jiffy says he didn't ever have a mother and that's funny "

"He had one You tell him he had one "

"He says he didn't, and he oughta know Says he just had a dad and he wasn't ever gonna have a mother 'cause him an' his dad don't want one I just as soon have one, though, if she was like my old mother Dad says he doesn't know about that, though " Raol jammed his hands down into the pockets of his overalls and scuffed his shoes on the dirt He looked from the ground to Jett and gave her a crooked grin "Well, I'll be going back now for some breakfast, Miss Black "

"You call me Jett," she said "Will you, Raol?"

"Sure " .

"And if you pass Luke—your dad—tell him I'm waiting for him, O K ?"

"O K , Jett," the boy answered He walked away slowly, touching the leaves on the bushes as he went along, and turning before he came to the trail to wave back at Jett as she sat watching him

When he was gone, Jett moved out from the tree into the sun She untied the straps of her halter and lay flat on her stomach, letting the warm rays tan her back. She could not help thinking of what Raol had said about his mother, feeling a slow, teasing jealousy mount inside her. Luke was the first man she had ever loved this way, and it occurred to her that she was not the only woman *he* had ever loved. What had his wife been like, and their life together? She realized she knew very little about Luke, and yet, except for the hazy jealous sensation at the mention of his wife, it did not seem to matter to Jett that Luke's past was unknown to her. The present mattered more, and the future most of all.

A slight rustle in the bushes arrested Jett's thinking. "Luke?"

Without rising, she tried to see, and saw only the greenness of the leaves and the brown color of the woods beyond. She imagined that it was undoubtedly a bird or a squirrel, and she let her head rest in her arms, and the sun's rays bathe her back.

Half consciously, she unstrapped her wrist watch and placed it at her side, settling back and closing her eyes, not thinking of anything, but feeling the warmth envelop her. She hoped that the weird summer weather Virginia was enjoying would stay throughout fall, and that winter would be short. During the cold months Bel Aire was less lively and Blake spent more time at the house. She had looked forward to that season before, knowing that it meant Blake, anticipating it eagerly. Now she dreaded it, not only because of Luke, but because it was suddenly an altogether different relationship she had with Blake. Jett was not sure that she could find things to talk about with him. He had always held her complete confidence and it was impossible to continue that way. Even their funny, private jokes would seem stale and idle, she knew, and both their humors were becoming brooding, each distrusting the other.

She heard the crunch of leaves, and she looked up again. "Luke?"

There was no answer, but she heard steps approaching and she called his name again. Her head raised just slightly above her arms, she could not see well, but she was sure it was he. She said, "I'm over here by the tree."

"I know where you're at," a voice answered. Two thick legs in muddy pants confronted her, and she shot up when she heard the voice, the halter falling down to her waist. Momentarily she stood paralyzed, face to face with Willie Kane, his eyes staring, not at her face, but at her breasts.

"I knew where you was, don't worry. I been watchin' yuh from the bushes," he said. His eyes did not leave her chest, and she backed away, fumbling with her halter, trying to fix the tie at her neck. He came closer, step by step, his hands extended as though he were trying to touch her.

"Let me see 'em," he said. "Let me look at 'em."

She watched his face, hating it, hating the thin edge of tongue at his lips, the glistening of his eyes, the way he moved to her. Her feet were like lead and she could only back up, almost painfully, away from him, her hands trying futilely to tie the straps together. He stopped a few feet away from her and shook with laughter, the laugh wheezy and harsh. With a dirty, thick hand he wiped his mouth and giggled harder, coughing and breathing hard.

"Never expected me, did yuh? Haw-w, yuh didn't think I was smart enough to git you out here when you was alone. I ain't gonna hurt yuh none. I'm just gonna touch yuh a little."

"Get away!" Jett found her voice as he came closer. "You get away!"

"You'll like me, you see, if I just git to put my hands on—"

Jett was near the end of the bank, unable to go farther, her feet not firm enough under her to run. Quickly she readied herself, and turning her back on him, she dived

down into the ring of water, her halter falling in the air
as she went. Coming to the surface, she saw him sliding
down the bank, grabbing the halter from the stones
where it had landed, his face red with excitement.

She treaded water after she swam a few yards out. Her
fear made her breathless, and her legs ached as they
moved.

"Look what I got!" he called out. "You want it. Lookit!" He held the halter up and laughed. "You gonna get
'em all cold in that water."

Jett made herself be calm. She caught her breath,
swimming over to a rock at the bank, a steep side where
he would not be able to go by foot. She held onto
the rock and rested while she watched him come as close
as he could get, the halter clutched in his hand.

"You're going to get beat up good for this!" She
screamed her words out, unable to remember when she
had ever been so filled with murder that it throbbed
through her legs and up to her temples.

"You ain't gonna tell," he called back.

"I'm going to tell plenty. You'll hang, you shriveled-up
idiot!"

"If you tell, missy, I tell too. I tell plenty too. Haw-w,
I seen you and your Mr. Hetherington up at yer place.
I been following yuh and I seen plenty to tell. Yer old
man don't know them things, betcha he don't, and I
kin tell him where an' when and how. Haw, I can tell
him how, too!"

"Liar!" The blood rushed to Jett's head as she held
to the rock, panting, trying to assemble the things he
had said. He had been following them! Her nails broke
on the rock and her thoughts spun while she cried, "Liar!"

He giggled, swaying back and forth, calling out more
threats between giggles, describing how he had seen them,
vulgarly, obscenely. His face writhed with peculiar pleasure, and his broken body heaved as he shouted at her.
Then he stopped, startled like an animal, and Jett lis-

tened and heard the vague sound of hoofbeats on the trail. She saw Willie Kane drop the halter, and like an animal scurry up the rocks, clawing them with his hands, slipping back now and then, but reaching the top at last. He was out of sight instantly, and Jett crawled from the water, held onto the jagged rock at the side of the cliff, and, exhausted, lay there shivering from the cold and the violent fear freezing in her heart.

It seemed an eternity before she heard Luke call from high above her.

"Jett! Jett!"

She could not answer him and he called louder. Trying to lift herself from the rocks, she fell back again. "Jett! God, what's happened, Jett?"

He was running, falling and slipping on the rocks as he came, reaching that part of the bank where he could go no farther on foot, and jumping into the water, fully clothed, splashing up behind to reach her.

"What happened? Jett!"

His soaking form crawled over to her, his hand touching hers. "Not Willie Kane!" he said.

She repeated the name. "Willie Kane."

"I saw him running along. I never— God, no! What'd he do, darling? God!"

"He didn't touch me," she managed to say. "He tried to but I jumped into the quarry. I— oh, Luke, he knows everything about us!"

"Come on," Luke said. "Let me help you to the top. This isn't the place to tell me. You're shivering. Let me help you."

He put his arms around her waist and pulled her down into the water with him, guiding her along to another part of the bank. When they reached the stones and started up, she saw her halter and picked it from the gray granite, holding it tightly in her fingers as Luke boosted her up the embankment from behind.

On level ground he put the towel around her shoulders

and sat her in the sun. His sweater and pants were wringing wet, and his feet squished inside his sneakers. "Try to
tell me," he said. "Take your time, but try to tell me
everything."

As he listened to her faltering words, he untied his
shoes and stripped off his sweater. Underneath his pants
he had a pair of worn trunks, the wool dripping from
his sudden swim. Jett took a while to tell her story, gasp-
ing for breath, shutting her eyes and shaking her head
back and forth as she talked, as though she were relating
a nightmare. When she was finished, Luke said, "The
damn fool! I'll sock his silly face in for him!"

"But don't you see? You can't!"

"What do you mean I can't?"

"I mean—then he *will* tell Blake."

"Listen, damn it, I'm going to tell Blake myself! Jett,
I'm tired of this kindergarten psychology you think you're
administering to your father for his welfare. For God's
sake, Jett, how far can you carry it?"

"You'll *never* understand, will you, Luke? You don't
know Blake at all and you *can't* understand! I hate Willie Kane worse and harder than I've ever hated anyone
in my life, but not enough to ruin Blake just because I'd
like to see Kane punched blue in the face. Ruin! That's
the word, Luke! That's what I'd do to Blake, and God
knows he's had enough happen to him."

Luke bent over her and gripped her shoulders. "Listen," he said. "Listen. This morning Vince walked up to
me. He handed me my cap. Didn't say anything, just
handed it to me and walked on. God! You'd think I was
a high-school kid dating behind my folks' backs. I thought
maybe Blake knew and I was glad. I thought it would be
swell if he knew. Because then we wouldn't have to act as
if we were doing something dirty behind someone's barn
door. Now I see it isn't that way. Vince was being the
silent hero of the drama, huh? That right?"

Jett said, "He saved our necks, Luke. He found your

cap yesterday under the couch and hid it before Blake saw it. We ought to thank our stars. Oh, but what's the use? You just can't see anything!"

"I see that I love you, Jett. Damn it, I love you, and—I want to marry you. I want to marry you, damn it! There's no law against that, is there? Or did Blake make a law against any man marrying his daughter?"

She put her arms on Luke's shoulders and let the impact of his words sink deep into her consciousness. Marriage. Indirectly, perhaps, subconsciously, perhaps, but never directly with full awareness had she thought of marrying Luke. Even her bravest pictures of the future during the past two weeks had somehow omitted the possibility of marriage—to Luke, to anyone. She thought inevitably of Blake, of announcing such news to him, imagining his reaction, his stark harrowing disbelief.

"I only know that I love you, Jett, and I only care about having you with me. Always having you with me." The words remembered then were ominous, and she could imagine Blake's hand gripping hers the way it had that night in his bedroom when he had told her that.

"Did you hear what I said, Jett?"

"Yes. Yes, Luke."

"It's a hell of a way to propose to a girl, but I had to blurt it out. You're young, honey, but you're no teen-ager. You're old enough to get married and settle down, and Jett, I love you. I think you love me too, honey. You've just got to—"

She said, "I love you, Luke. But—"

"No buts! I'm going to Blake and tell him. Why, I'll bet he'll be glad to get you off his hands."

Blake would kill Luke! Crippled or strong, he would kill him, and then die himself, inside.

Jett took her hands from Luke's shoulders. She looked away, off to the bushes and the forest of brown trees. "No, Luke," she said emphatically, "you're not going to tell Blake. If you do, I'll never see you again. I know

Blake, and I love him. There are some things outsiders can't judge—haven't got the right to judge. I came here this morning to talk with you—to tell you I didn't want to see you again like this until Blake was well. He's down now. I wanted to wait. Heaven knows it'd be hell on my nerves, but I wanted to do the right thing. I don't like running behind his back any more than you do, and yesterday, when Vince found the cap, I knew we couldn't afford to do it any more. When Blake got better, I thought we'd let him know gradually, easily, so it wouldn't jolt him suddenly, but grow on him until he got accustomed to it. The way you want to do it, you'll kill all three of us."

Luke put his hands around her waist, facing her back. His voice had a tone of incredulity. "Didn't you hear what I said, Jett? About us getting married?"

The feel of his hands on her body stirred her. She would not look at him, but kept her eyes fixed ahead of her. She could not give in—not if she was to keep him—but she felt herself losing him, involuntarily, almost naturally losing him. Marriage? Why not marriage? she thought. After Blake got well, why not? Luke and she could live at Bel Aire. Blake never denied that Luke was the best man he had on the farm. She would not really be leaving Blake any more than she had already left him. She would still be with him, and Luke would be her husband.

"Listen," she said. "Listen, Luke." She turned around and held onto him, the wet towel on her shoulders pressing against his skin, her eyes meeting his fully for the first time that morning. "We will marry! We will! I want to marry you, Luke. God, I never thought of it. It's crazy but I never thought of it! Why, a few hours ago I was talking with Raol and he was telling me he wanted a mother. He said—" She laughed recalling the way the boy had worded it. "He said he'd just as soon have another mother."

Luke laughed too and his arms encircled her. "He'd be crazy about you, Jett."

"We *can* get married. It won't be long. Blake's going to New York and the doctors there are sure to cure him. We'll see each other when he's gone, and even sometimes when I can sneak away and meet you here and we can talk—"

Luke interrupted her. His blue eyes were fierce with a quick fury and he pushed her back, glaring at her, his chin thrust forward stubbornly.

"When are you going to wake up?" he said. "When are you going to stop living in that merry-go-round make-believe world you hide in! Jett, your father is paralyzed, damn it! He's permanently paralyzed! Only a miracle's going to get him well, and I don't believe in miracles! I never did and I don't now! If we have to wait for Blake to get well, we'll be in our graves quicker than we'll ever be married!"

Jett shouted back at him, "Don't talk that way!"

"Ask Vince if you won't believe me. Vince said the Richmond doctor said Blake was a hopeless case! Hopeless!"

"You're lying!"

"Ask him! Ask Vince!"

Jett got to her feet, throwing the towel on the ground and reaching down for her shirt and pants. She pulled them on while Luke sat looking up at her, and she said nothing to him. Her hair was still wet from the quarry water, and she pushed it back behind her ears. Stooping to retrieve the towel, she rung the drops of water from it and rolled it up, stuffing it under her arm.

"I'm telling you the truth, Jett," Luke said calmly. "I think you know in your heart that I'm telling you the truth."

She stared at him and it was as though she had never seen his face before. She no longer wanted to believe that he was Luke, that he was the man she loved.

"I don't believe that," she said. "Blake's never lied to me. He said there was hope. There *has* to be hope. I'll believe in him, in his ability to get strong again, as long as I believe in the fact that I'm alive."

Luke shrugged his shoulders and turned his head away from her. "Then forget it," he said. "Might as well forget it."

He did not watch her go, but heard the horse whinny as Jett rode him away, and he sat on the earth above the water listlessly, his fingers digging in the soft dirt beside him. Kane was driving a shipment to Raleigh at eleven. It would be an opportunity to get away for a few hours, and Willie Kane would not be able to drive anyway. Not after Luke finished with him. He stood up, his eyes suddenly alert and purposeful, his fists clenched.

Chapter Sixteen

AFTER LUNCH, Blake wheeled his way across the yard from the mess shack to the office building. He kept remembering breakfast with Jett, her detached answers to his questions, her black hair damp, and her placid explanation that she had felt warm when she awakened, and had decided to go for a swim at the quarry. Blake did not want the thoughts he had, but he could not prevent them from harrying him. Hetherington was the only person at Bel Aire that Blake had ever known to use the quarry for swimming, and even at noon the day was not hot, but cool. Yesterday he had been willing to blame himself for his sick musings and vain suspicions of Jett and Luke Hetherington, attributing them to his own feeble brooding, and detesting himself for allowing them to take root in his mind. But today, this morning, and now as he made his way back to the office, he was almost positive that these suppositions were valid. It was not Jett he blamed, but Hetherington. Luke Hetherington was ostensibly tranquil and unallied with other people, a silent man who performed his tasks well and did not interfere with the lives of the men around him. Behind this mask of independence, Blake was sure Luke hid his true nature, a maliciously selfish one, predatory and mean. If there were anything to woman's intuition, then Jett had been right in the early days when Luke was hired. She had told Blake then that Luke Hetherington was intent on robbing Blake of everything he possessed. Jett was his only real possession, Blake thought ironically, and Hetherington was drawing her into his scheme, taking advantage of her youth and of Blake's incapacity. If he could only be sure of that, Blake would banish him in an hour's time, but he was not sure.

As he rounded the corner and struggled with the wheels of his chair on the slate walk, he saw Willie Kane hobbling across the green lawn to meet him.

Willie could still feel the pain at his ribs where Luke had hit him and kicked him, cursing at him and threatening to kill him. Well, he'd get even, he would. He'd fix the lot of them with their noses in the air, treating him like he was no better than a dog. Lord, the pain when he walked!

"Mr. Black! Hey, Mr. Black!"

Blake stopped and waited for him to come over, pitying his knotted body and gnarled face. At the same time, Blake disliked dealing with the man in any way at all, having to watch him when he spoke and hear the warped sound of his voice. Willie was out of breath, and his mouth had saliva at the corners, which he wiped off on his sleeve before he began, whispering in a gruff overtone, his hands rubbing each other to give the coarse sound like sandpaper working on smooth wood. His eyes were small and bright like a snake's eyes.

"I gotta talk to yuh. I gotta tell yuh somethin'."

"Go ahead."

"Not here."

"I said, go ahead. I can talk here."

Willie's parched lips divided in a round grin. "Not about this, uh-uh. Naw." He tittered and licked his lips. "Office," he said. "Office."

Blake swore to himself and pushed the wheels along the walk while Kane followed. "Might as well begin," he said as he went down the walk. "Couldn't be that big a secret."

"Wait and you see. Tell yuh when we git to the office."

Willie squinted over his back to see if anyone saw them. Hetherington had taken the truck to Raleigh, but Willie was afraid of *her*. If she saw him with Mr. Black, he'd get another whipping, and he might not get up and walk after that one. Hell, he didn't care. He'd show the lot of

them. He laughed aloud and saw Blake Black turn and
glare at him and then turn back and push his wheel chair
farther. Let him stare, damn him. He'd get his ears full,
he would, damn him and that daughter of his. Someday
he'd give it to her the way he wanted to. By God, someday he'd get that one with her dark hair and her dancing
body. He bit his lip and slouched after Blake's wheel
chair.

"All right, Kane," Blake said, turning the chair around
and facing him inside the office. "What do you want?
And why are you coming to me about it? Hetherington's
the one you should go to."

"Can't go to him, naw—not fer this, Mr. Black." Willie
shifted his weight to his other foot and stuck his hands in
his pockets. He was going to tell him, all right. The pain
in his back was going away, but he was going to tell him,
because goddamn! Goddamn!

"Out with it!" Blake's impatience gave Willie the
creeps. Why was he impatient when Willie was going to
tell him in just a minute? He didn't like to look at Willie,
that was why. He didn't like to see his back all hunched
over and ugly. Him and all the other people. He'd fix
them for being so straight!

"You wanna know bout Miss Jett and him? Hetherington? You wanna know what they do t'gether when you
ain't around 'em? I know. You—"

"What are you saying?" Blake thundered. "What the
hell are you trying to say?"

Willie backed away. "Lookit, I seen 'em. I ain't lying.
I seen 'em and I tell her I'm comin' to yuh and tell yuh
and she say I'm a liar, but she knows what I'm talkin'
about. She and that Mr. Luke know."

Blake cornered Willie with his wheel chair, pushing
him over by the window, his words barely spat out from
between his teeth. "What are you telling me? What are
you saying to me?"

"I seen 'em once up at the house. You was away. You

was in Richmond and I seen 'em through the window. I seen—"

"You—" Blake stopped and brought his fist down hard on the arm of his chair.

"An' they was at the quarry this mornin'. I seen 'em there and they was doing the same thing out there and—"

"Shut up!"

Willie's lips trembled and his back was against the windowpane, his hands in front of him, palms up, afraid of Blake Black, afraid Black would reach for him. But Blake just sat there staring at the floor, his eyes shut, silent for minutes before he looked up at Willie.

He said, "You're lying."

"Naw. I seen it. I seen it!"

"You're lying, Kane!"

"I ain't. I tell who what I seen. I told her I was gonna tell yuh."

Blake shook his head and jammed his hands in his coat pocket. The quarry! The quarry made it true! She *was* at the quarry that morning.

Willie said, "Mr. Luke, he going to kill me. He say he'll kill me."

"Does he know you're telling me this?"

"Naw. He gone to Raleigh. Took my job, he did. I was supposed to go and he socked me and then he went. He try to kill me with his fists an' kickin' me an'—"

"Jett! Does *she* know you're here now?"

"Naw. Naw. No one. I come here myself. I tell 'em I was comin' but they don't believe me."

"Hetherington tried to kill you before you got to me, huh?"

"Yeah," Willie said. "Yeah." He was pleased now. Blake was acting the way he wanted him to. He'd show them. Them two!

"Listen," Blake said. "You listen to me, Kane. Don't you tell them you came here. Don't you tell anyone you came here. Do you understand that? No one!"

"Naw, I won't. I won't."

Willie's eyes shone and he giggled, but Blake said, "Get that stinking laugh out of you, now. Get it off your blubbering mouth! Now listen, tell me what you saw. Everything you saw. And if you tell anyone you were here, I'll let them kill you! I'll help them!"

"I won't," Willie said. He bent over Blake's wheel chair and his thick voice started, rising as he related what he had seen, word for word, the pictures clear in his mind, his fingers itching as he talked, a hammer pounding inside him as he told Blake everything.

Blake planned to wait until after dinner, when they had their coffee in the living room. Jett had been unusually quiet during the meal, and as Blake sat across from her he tried to read her mind, to read his interpretation of her thoughts into the frown on her forehead. The kitchen table had been set attractively, the cool blue linen cloth matching Jett's silk dress with the candy-stripe design, and the meal had been elaborate, hours of care taken to prepare it. In this way she had been atoning, Blake decided, for the lies and flimsy excuses that she had used to pass over her relationship with Luke Hetherington. He would make sure that he was right before he took any action, because Blake knew that when he did, he would act violently. Hetherington would pay dearly for his attempt at winning Jett, and if Jett was as susceptible to him as Willie Kane had pictured it, she too would reap her share of punishment. She was young, too young, and too beautiful for her own good. But the years would heal any bruise administered now, and Blake would not let her come that close to it again. He had thought of its happening before. As recently as three months ago he had thought of the possibility of Jett's meeting a man whom she might fall in love with—someday. Since his accident he had shoved the thought far back in his mind, damned it, condemned it. He would give her more than any man could ever give her, and a man like Hetherington would only hurt her, use her for his own selfish purposes and then discard her. Blake wondered what Hetherington had done to his wife, under what circumstances she had died, and why Luke Hetherington had never told him about her. She must have been a victim of his perverted desire to possess for the sake of possessing, just as Jett would be if Blake had not learned the truth. . . . *Was* it the truth? He had to know soon—tonight!

Jett looked up and smiled at Blake. "Coffee, Bunny? You've been so quiet."

"We've both been caught up in our own thoughts, I guess." Blake pushed his chair back from the table. "Yes, coffee will taste good. I'll wait in the living room for it."

If what Willie Kane had said *was* true, Jett would be afraid of him now. She did not know that Kane had already told him everything, and she would be haunted by the fear that he would do just that. Blake scratched a match on the folder and put it to the cigarette in his mouth as he sat in the living room glancing idly about him. This room where he had known so much happiness with Jett. And this room where Willie Kane had said he saw them! Blake winced and blew the smoke through his nostrils, watching it spiral up into the air and drift away lazily.

When Jett carried the tray with the coffee cups balanced on it into the room, Blake studied her beauty, longing for some miraculous intervention that would wake him out of the nightmare he was living. Her narrow ankles held the leather straps of her high heels, and a frivolous lace petticoat showed a bare inch below the hemline of her dress. She always used to change into a fresh outfit for their evening meals, surprising him each time with her dazzling appeal, her facility for appearing more and more beautiful every day. She had neglected this in the past month, but tonight the custom was renewed, and Blake regretted that he thought he knew why

Jett did it. Her guilt was apparent now, he decided, and he had only to hear it from her own lips. To hear her say that it was true.

"Sugar and cream, and there you are." She handed him the cup and smiled, settling herself on the divan and taking her own cup from the coffee table.

"Jett, I'm thinking of making a few changes around the farm."

"Oh? I guess it could use some."

"Yes, I think certain ideas you had from the very beginning—after my accident—were good ideas."

He would have to take it slowly, he realized, so that he could see her reactions from the moment they began until they grew to the point where he could be positive. He stirred his coffee and squashed his cigarette out in the ash tray at his side.

"What ideas were those?"

Blake looked at her. Her face was relaxed, and her eyes did not seem upset or nervous. She was a brilliant actress, brilliant and awesome.

"Well, for one thing, I haven't been satisfied with our shipments. They aren't on time, and they're done in a sloppy way. The horses look like hell when they reach their destination."

"How do you know that?"

"The buyers have complained, for one thing, and Jenkins down at Firth track tells me he never ceases to wonder that the yearlings get there at all."

"Jenkins!" Jett said. "Since when has *his* word meant anything?"

It was true that Jenkins was a drunkard, unreliable and foolish. Blake had made up the story, but he knew that in the past Jett would have been in accord with Jenkins or anyone else who wanted to criticize something she had previously criticized. And previously, she had called Willie Kane an idiot, incapable of doing anything intelligently. Surely she knew now that Blake meant to attack

Kane. Yet she was denying that there could be anything wrong with Kane's handling of the shipments.

"Besides," Jett said, "most of our men are familiar with the routine here. If we get new workers, we'll have to break them in all over again."

"Willie Kane isn't so familiar with anything. He's only been here a short time."

Blake saw her lower her eyes as she raised the coffee to her lips and sipped it carefully.

"I thought you were the one that insisted Kane stay on," she said.

"I can make a mistake."

"I don't see the sense of changing drivers. One's as good as the next." She finished the coffee and placed it on the tray, looking over at Blake, and a little more earnestly she said, "I know he's a jackass, and he looks like Frankenstein, but I can't see that he's doing any real harm, Bunny."

"You used to hate him."

"I used to hate a lot of things. I don't know. I—I really don't think he's done anything to be fired for."

She *was* afraid. Her hands clasped together as she sat talking, and there was an urgency in her answers, in her defense of Willie Kane.

"Of course," Blake said, "if you don't want me to fire him, I won't."

She said, "I don't see why you should."

"Then you don't want me to?"

"No," she said, "I guess I don't. Let's wait, Bunny. Everything will work out O.K."

"I hope you're right, Cricket." He leaned back and thought of what he must do, knowing that it was the only way, the only way for him to do it.

"What other changes were you thinking of making?" she said.

Blake reached in his pocket for another cigarette and waited while Jett struck the match for him and held it up. He touched her hand briefly until the flame caught the tobacco.

"I think I'll let them go for now," he said. "I have to go away."

"Really?"

"Yes, I'll be gone overnight. Tomorrow," Blake said. "I plan to leave tomorrow."

The room in the bunkhouse was thick with smoke and the smell of canned beer. A radio played low on the bench near the window and the three men at the card table yelled out through the door.

"Hurry it up!"

"C'mon! C'mon!"

Vince stood in the hall talking through the odd-shaped black phone with the hose neck.

"Sure, but why all of a sudden?" he said.

He could not hear well above the jeers of the poker game, and he put one hand to his free ear and shouted, "I said O.K. O.K. if you want it that way. . . . What?"

Someone had turned the radio on full blast and Vince shouted in at them, muffling the neck of the phone with his hand, "Shut up, you fools! It's the boss!"

Instantly the radio was snapped off and the noise stopped. "Yes, I heard you," Vince said. "Tomorrow afternoon. Five. All right."

He hung the ear back on the hook and stood leaning against the wall.

Now, why the hell, he said to himself, does he want to drive to Richmond again? And to start at five in the afternoon!

"Hey, Vince! Hurry it up!"

Vince cursed Blake and walked back to the smoky room to pick up his cards and make his bid.

Chapter Seventeen

SHE WAITED until they were out of sight, until the car took the bend in the dirt road beyond the farm. Hurriedly she ran to the corner of the room, picked up the telephone, and dialed the three numbers that rang the mess. She asked for him and waited. In the background on the other end of the wire she could hear the noise of the men talking, laughing, the rattling of plates, the sound of running water. Week nights the men ate early, between five-thirty and six, and there was a remote chance that Luke might be there. Jett preferred to talk with him on the phone to ask him to come to the house, rather than go down to the farm and seek him out. They could have dinner together—fry up the chicken she had in the freezer.

"Yes? . . . Oh. Well, do you know where he is? . . . I see. Thanks," she said, placing the phone back in its cradle. The man had said that Hetherington rarely ate at the mess, that he cooked for himself over in the cabin. She should have known that, but sometimes it was hard for her to remember Raol. There was no phone in the cabin. She would have to go there herself.

At the mirror in the hall Jett paused, tucked the white sweater into her dark skirt, and strapped the wide kid belt around her waist. She kicked her loafers off and went into the bedroom to get a pair of low-heeled white play shoes. Sitting on the bed, she tied them at her ankles, and paused momentarily to wonder just what she would say to Luke, how she would say it.

"Luke, I don't think we've talked about it enough." That sounded cold and matter-of-fact, as though they were discussing business. She would have to think of some other way to put it, some way to make him receptive.

In the pocket of the skirt she wore, she found a lipstick and comb. She went back to the mirror and unscrewed the top of the lipstick, putting the faint red color on her lips lightly, pressing them together, and then standing back to see herself. She ran the comb through her hair, smoothed her skirt, and straightened the sweater again, tightening the belt another notch. Then she reached up to the hook in the closet and took her suede jacket to place around her shoulders. After a final look, she snapped off the bright light and walked through to the kitchen and out the door.

From the hill she could see a boy leading the horses in from the field, and the chimney on the mess shack was sending up streams of gray smoke into the damp air, damp from the early-afternoon rain. She had not been at the farm all day, knowing that Blake would be gone after five, and that if she were to see Luke at all, she would see him then. The thought of Willie Kane bothered her and she quickened her pace, afraid that he might be near. She would use that in her argument with Luke, if there was an argument, as an excuse for his returning with her to the house. It would not be entirely false, for she *was* afraid of Kane. She did not know what she feared most—the chance that he might try to attack her again, or the chance that he might go to Blake and tell him about Luke and herself. It was lucky, she thought as she walked, that Blake had told her about his idea of firing Willie. If Willie *had* been fired, he would be sure to tell Blake then. Jett wondered how Blake would have reacted. Doubtless he would have thought Kane was a liar, but the seed would be planted, and Jett felt she could not afford that.

Jiffy was wandering through the fields with a net when Jett reached the bottom of the hill. She smiled to herself, recalling Raol's excitement over the proposition of catching field mice. If Raol were in the cabin with Luke, she would tell him that she had passed Jiffy, encouraging him to leave Luke and her alone. Maybe she should ask the boy for dinner too, she thought. She could talk with Luke after dinner. Perhaps he would stay all night. They had never slept in a bed together. It had always been unplanned, haphazard. The prospect made Jett eager to be with him, to make him see, somehow, that it was not over just because they had to wait. Once he heard that Blake had gone to Richmond to see another doctor, he might change his mind about Blake's chances of getting well.

There was a light shining from the small window in the front of the cabin. As she went up the walk, Jett could not see Luke or Raol, but she went on to the door, which was closed, and knocked lightly.

"Hi, Miss Black. We're eating dinner." Raol stood before her, holding the screen door open with one hand, a fork in the fingers of his other hand. He had a long paper napkin tucked into the polo shirt at his neck.

"I'm sorry to interrupt," she said. "Shall I come back?"

"I don't know, but the flies are—"

Luke's voice rang out. "Come in."

The table was over in a corner of the room, a checkered plastic cloth covering it, two plates laden with baked beans set on it, with a round dish filled with applesauce in the center. Jett looked at Luke, at the way he sat there, his legs straddling the sides of the chair, the soiled tan work shirt ripped at the neck, his big hands reaching for the bread on the empty chair between his and Raol's.

"Sit down," he said. "Eaten yet?"

Matter-of-fact and simple, the way she had been afraid to be. Luke was that way, always. There was not even a slight hint of their bitter words the day before; nothing but a plain, crude invitation to dinner. Jett smiled at him, a wide smile, flooded with the love that she was so sure of then, and she sat down in the chair.

"Pass the lady the beans," Luke said to Raol, and he winked at Jett, grinned, and dug his fork into his food.

The Blue Mill Restaurant was the sole serious restaurant in Hillsboro. The others served rubbery hamburgers along with the mugs of draught beer, but they took no pains to make the food attractive. Their money came from the liquor trade, and from the countless mugs and bottles of beer that passed across their counters nightly. At The Blue Mill, Ike Conover cooked his dishes carefully, taking pride in his version of Italian spaghetti and lasagna, as well as his wife's famed Irish stews. Hillsboro folks patronized him regularly when they ate out, and Ike served them royally, hyperconscious of little things like ash trays, empty water glasses, and spotted table cloths. He could always count on the bar trade, and he let Pat handle all of that, but the "eatin' customers" got his personal attention.

He couldn't remember ever having Blake Black for an "eatin' customer" since he'd been in business these fifteen-odd years. Young Gellert came in from the farm on occasion, but Blake never did. Ike hurried over to their table to clear the dishes and ask them how they liked the dinner. He was disappointed to find Blake's dish three quarters full.

"Something the matter with the clam sauce, Mr. Black?" Ike's bald head caught the reflection of the soft blue lights around the walls, and his gray eyes searched Blake's for an answer to his question.

The answer was offhand, brushed aside. "All right," Blake said. "Was all right."

Ike's thin form hovered over the table. "I like my customers to be satisfied. Can't rightly call you a real customer, Mr. Black, but just the same I—"

Blake interrupted. "I said it was all right! Get me another Scotch and water!"

"Yes, sir!" Ike snapped to attention and began clearing the table in a businesslike manner, but his eyes had that offended look, his forehead drooped with depression. Vince muttered something Ike could not hear and then he addressed Ike suddenly. "The meal was swell, Ike! Really swell! Mr. Black just isn't hungry tonight."

"Don't make excuses for me!" Blake said sharply. "Nobody has to make excuses for me."

Ike was glad to leave the table, balancing the dishes on his arm, hurrying off to the bar to give Pat the drink order. He did not know Blake Black very well, but he felt angry, hurt and angry, at the way the man had treated him. Up at his farm he could treat people that way all he wanted to, but it was different at The Blue Mill. Folks came there to enjoy the food and relax and talk a spell, and Blake Black wasn't that kind of folks. He was a pompous old outsider, and Ike didn't wonder that Hillsboro didn't like him. Many a night he'd listened to the men at the bar talk about Black, call him every name in the book, and Ike had thought at the time that no one could be that bad. No one. But maybe Blake Black deserved it, Ike thought as he banged the dishes down in the sink in back. By God, he *did* deserve it, acting high and mighty that way.

"I don't get it," Vince was saying to Blake. "I don't get it at all! It's seven o'clock now. We're not going to make Richmond tonight."

Blake smirked and lighted a cigarette. "Where's my drink? This is some restaurant, this is!"

"Nobody asked you to come here! God, Blake, you act like you were doing them a favor. Ike takes pride in this place, and you—"

"Aw, cut it out! Cut out the sermon, Vince."

Vince's jaw tightened, and his hand under the table made a tight ball that whitened his knuckles. "I'm not going to drive all night, Blake. You're going too far this time. I'm not going to drive all night to Richmond just because you have a whim to get loaded before we take off!"

"If you like Ike so well, maybe you'd like to work for him and quit working for me. You wouldn't have to do

any driving then. You could wrestle with dirty spaghetti
dishes and mop up floors. Haw. The great accountant!"

"What *is* the matter with you tonight?" Vince sat forward and stared at Blake's surly face. "What in the
name of God is the trouble with you?"

"I feel like having another drink. Does something have
to be the matter with a man when he wants a drink?"

Ike came across the room carrying the single glass.
Gingerly he set it down in front of Blake and waited,
looking at Vince.

"No, thanks, Ike."

"Whyn't you have one?" Blake said. "Bring him one."

"I said I didn't want one!"

"Bring him one anyway, and if he doesn't drink it, I
will."

Shrugging his shoulders, Ike gave Vince a helpless look
and went back to the bar. Vince's face flamed, and he
brought his fist from under the table and held it to his
chest in a gesture of unbearable anger.

"If you weren't a cripple, I'd—" As soon as he had said
the words he despised the wrath that had forced them out.
Blake's face broke, the lines of his forehead shrinking, his
mouth collapsing open, his eyes wrinkling. He was silent
a moment, and then wetting his lips he spoke huskily.
"That's right. If I weren't a cripple . . . if I weren't a
cripple a lot of things would be different, wouldn't they?
People would feel different. The whole world would
be different. Did y'know it changed, Vince? Overnight!
Changed overnight when I landed in this goddamn kiddy
cart! World got different! If I weren't a cripple it wouldn't
have happened. But I am a cripple, damn it. I'm a cripple, Vince. I am."

"I'm sorry, Blake. I'm sorry I said it."

Blake gulped his drink down. A farmer walked over to
the pin-ball machine at the back of the restaurant and
shoved a nickel in the slot. The lights colored on the
board behind, and the farmer punched the lever and let

the balls run through the alleys. Bells rang, and the sound of the balls falling back in the case sounded heavy.

Vince took a deep breath and looked back at Blake. "What about it, Blake? We better get started."

"They don't help cripples in Richmond. You know that."

"Look, Blake," Vince said, "if you want to go there to see a doctor, I'll be glad to drive you. I want you to get better. You ought to know that. It's a long trip and you'll need to be rested for an examination. We better leave now."

Blake laughed. He raised the empty tumbler to his lips trying to swallow another drink, and laughed. "We're not going to Richmond, Vince."

"We can still make it, Blake."

"Listen, you fool," Blake said. "We're not going and we were never going! You take me for a nincompoop? Just because I'm crippled you think I'd start off for Richmond at five in the afternoon? You think I'm out of my head?"

The pin-ball machine rang out several times and the lights spelled out "Score." The old farmer chuckled and turned to see who was watching him. He slammed another nickel in the slot, still chuckling.

"Then what in the name of God is this all about?"

"It's about Jett! This is about Jett. Get me another drink, Vince."

Vince ignored the order. "Jett! What do you mean?"

"I said get me another drink!"

Ike heard Blake's shout and he hurried to Pat, and rushed back to the table with another tumbler and a shot glass. Blake caressed the glass and smiled. "Yeah, it's about Jett. My little girl."

"You're getting drunk, Blake."

"I got reason to. I never had better reason to."

"What about Jett? What crazy scheme are you hatching?" Vince knew. He knew the moment Blake mentioned

Jett's name. He was not sure of Blake's plan, but he knew it involved Luke Hetherington.

"What time is it, Vince?"

"Seven-thirty."

"We've got to wait. We've got to wait an hour or two."

It was clear to Vince then. Blake planned to go back to the house and surprise Jett. He hoped to have a chance to catch the two of them together.

"I'm not going with you," Vince said. "I'm not going to have any part in this."

"In what? What the hell do you know?"

"In whatever you're planning."

"Seems like everyone knew but me. You knew, too, didn't you?"

"You're talking crazy. I don't know what you're talking about," Vince said.

"About Hetherington! You know damn well what's been going on, don't you?"

"You're so drunk you don't know what you're saying, Blake!"

"Don't you know about it?"

"I don't know a thing about it!" Vince said. "I only know you're full of a lot of lousy suspicions. I knew it the other afternoon when you hiked up to the house to see if Hetherington was there with Jett. You could have called, but you didn't. You wanted to catch her in the act, or him. I don't know what you wanted to do. No, Blake, I don't know a damn thing. But I do know this: You act as if she were your slave—as if she didn't have any right to be attracted to a man—as if she couldn't live a normal life or you'd kill her for it! What's the matter with you? It makes me sick!"

The farmer scored again. He gave a whoop of delight and stamped his feet, the old wooden floor boards vibrating in the small room of the restaurant. Blake seemed not to hear. He reached for the glass in front of him and drank it dry. The farmer came over to the table with a big, toothless smile and asked them to change a quarter. Vince fumbled for change in his pocket, but Blake did not look at the man. His red eyes stared at the empty glass, his head nodding drunkenly. "Vincent," he said, "get me 'nother drink. Hell, we been talking too much. Tell them to bring me one more, Vincent!"

At the corner of Foote Street the high circular clock gonged eight times, and the men loitering outside the pool hall saw the tall, lean figure approaching slowly.

"That's him, ain't it?" one said. "First time I seen him up close."

"Him, all right," another said.

A third man spat into the gutter and rattled the loose change in his pants pocket. "Looks tired, don't he? No soft job working up there for that one."

They grew silent as Luke approached them. He wore the worn jeans, the same tan shirt with the rip at the neck, the skullcap, and the high work shoes that hit his legs just above the ankles. His head was bent, his eyes studying the cracks in the sidewalk. He walked as though he were oblivious of everything and everyone around him, his hands stuffed into his pockets, walking at an amble, scuffing the toes of his shoes as he went. When he passed the pool hall he looked up and in at the lights, then to the other side, where the men were congregated. His smile was stiff and unhappy.

"Fine evening," a man said to him. Luke nodded and kept on walking.

The man snickered and punched a companion in the ribs. "The whole bunch of 'em's in town t'night! All look nuts, don't they? Next thing you know, the girl'll be swinging along right b'fore our eyes. Bel Aire! Keep 'em, I say! You can keep 'em!"

Luke had left her in front of the cabin a half hour ago. He was not sure why he had walked into Hillsboro, but he was sure that he had to get away from the farm—from her. He had just started to walk, and before he knew it the dirt road broke into pavement and he saw the city lights, the stores, and the fireplugs at the corners. It was his first trip into town, but now that he was here he did not notice the town itself, or the people he passed, or the direction he walked. His mind was filled and brimming over with Jett, with what had been said between them, with the terrible ache for her, and with the futility.

Supper had gone well. Raol and Jett and he had laughed, eaten heartily, and talked easily. When Luke had heard her voice at the door he had thought that she was there because she had changed her mind. He had curbed the excitement in himself and let the first hour go its own way. Raol chattered on endlessly, spilling the applesauce over the floor of the cabin, gobbling his food, and directing all of his conversation to Jett. She answered him enthusiastically, her laughter spontaneous, her face beautiful in its natural radiance. Occasionally Luke's eyes met hers, the spark igniting between them, the look long, meaningful. He had been so sure.

When Raol left, after dinner, to hunt up Jiffy, Luke went to her, felt her arms at his waist, her lips cool, receiving his. They did not talk right away, but stayed together like that, their strength and weakness merged, their want imperative.

"I couldn't have stayed away, Luke. I couldn't have."

"It's going to be O.K. now."

"Will you come to the house with me? Tonight? Now?"

"Yes," he said. "Now."

"Blake's gone to Richmond. He won't be back until tomorrow."

Luke knew then that nothing had changed. He had misunderstood everything. For a crazy minute he had thought she wanted him to go with her to tell Blake about them. Instead, it was the same frantic plan to steal an-

other piece of time when they could be together unknown
to her father. No matter how much he wanted her then,
he would not let her come to him on such terms. He had
turned his back on her, seeing the table there with the
dirty dishes on it, the leftover food, Raol's unfinished
glass of milk, the crumbs on the plastic cloth, all needing
to be cleaned up, brushed away, and put back. Jett and
he were like that table, and Luke could not see why it
was not just as simple to resolve their own problem as
it was to tidy the table up after a meal. She was making
it hard, impossible, he thought, impossible!

"Did you hear me, Luke?"

"I heard you."

"Well, I'll help you and then we can go up to the
house."

"I'll go up to the house with you, Jett. I'll go up with
you when your father comes back from Richmond, to tell
him about us. That's the only time I'll go up there with
you."

"But don't you see? He *has* got a chance, Luke. He
wouldn't keep going to see the doctor if he didn't have a
chance. Blake isn't built that way. It'll just be a little
longer, Luke. I'll tell him then, I swear I will. Listen,
Luke, try to understand about Blake and me."

Crossing the street, Luke walked into the drugstore
and asked for a package of cigarettes. A row of hot dogs
was sizzling on the open grill, and the coffee was bubbling
in the large glass pot. The clerk who handed him the
change smiled coyly and said, "You're a stranger, aren't
you?" Her lipstick was eaten away and her dress was too
tight. She wore thick glasses, which she yanked off when
she looked at Luke, and she passed her dirty hands
through her hair, the odor of perspiration stifling as her
arm rose. Luke grunted and picked up the pennies she
had dropped on the counter.

"Still water runs deep, I always say." The girl gave a
high, hysterical laugh as Luke made his way out of the

drugstore into the street. He saw the car then. It was parked in front of The Blue Mill, and Luke walked closer, staring at it. It was Blake's car, all right. Hesitating, Luke peered in through the window of the restaurant, looked down the bar at the men standing there, and saw them sitting in the booth near the middle of the restaurant, Vince and Blake. He stuck a cigarette in his mouth, lighted it, and opened the screen door.

Pat passed a beer across the counter at Luke, and a fellow standing next to him made room for Luke to stand there. Luke took a swallow and saw the pair through the mirror. They were arguing, Vince angry and upset, Blake sullen and drunk. Luke did not understand it. He swallowed the rest of the beer, called for another, and walked over to the table.

"Good evening," he said.

At the sound of his voice, Blake's neck jerked and his black eyes needled Luke. He had a mask of incredulity over his face, a look of near horror. It startled Luke, and he looked away from Blake to Vince.

"Hi," Vince said. "How are you, Hetherington?"

"Fine. I saw you two over here and I thought I'd ask you to have a drink on me."

Vince said, "I think we've had enough for one night."

Blake was still piercing Luke with his eyes. Luke ran his finger along his collar and said something about the weather, but Blake's desperate oath broke into his words. "God!" Blake said. "God help me!"

"I think we better go home now," Vince said to him. "What do you think?"

Blake grabbed the tablecloth in his hand as he pushed his wheel chair back. Vince tore Blake's hand away from the cloth, steadied him by holding the back of his coat. "Easy," he said. He signaled to Ike to bring the check.

"I'll be seeing you," Luke said. He walked back to the bar and watched them from there. He saw Vince wheel Blake out of the restaurant, Blake making no effort to wheel the chair himself, as he usually did. Outside, Vince opened the car door, lifted Blake, and shoved him in the front seat. The wheel chair folded and Vince crammed it in the back seat. He slammed the door shut again and came back inside the restaurant, walking over to Ike, reaching inside his coat for his wallet and talking with Ike in a low voice.

"Sorry to cut you short," Vince said to Luke on his way out. "He's too much for anyone tonight."

"You're not going to drive to Richmond with him like that?"

Vince bit his lip and breathed a sigh before he answered. "Look, Hetherington," he said. "I don't like minding other people's business, but sometimes a guy can get all tangled up in it without meaning to. Blake had some kind of notion you'd be with Jett tonight. He was planning to surprise you both. The guy's not just crippled in his *body*, if you know what I mean. When you came in here it knocked him for a loop. He'll think he was all screwed up about that notion now, and hate himself for getting it in the first place." Vince paused and looked at Luke. He said, "I don't know whether that's good or bad, Hetherington, but I'm fed up with Blake Black. Good and fed up!"

The screen door banged after Vince, and the roar of the car motor started. Ike Conover mopped his brow with a large square handkerchief. He stood near the window shaking his head, and then, turning away, he shuffled back toward the kitchen.

"You'll need help!" Vince told Jett at the kitchen door. He lifted the wheel chair backward up the steps and brought it in through the door. Wheeling it around so that Blake faced Jett, Vince stepped back and looked at him. Blake's eyes squeezed and opened, and his hand came to his head, rubbing the temples, squinting in the light. Then he saw her, dressed in her robe, her black hair falling about her shoulders, her eyes tender with concern as she ran to him and took his hand. "Bunny, Bunny, what's the matter, honey?"

Blake's shoulders convulsed. His whole body throbbed, and his hands covered his face. He sat there crying, the thick sound of his sobs slicing the frozen silence as Jett watched, stricken with fear for him.

"Get him into the bedroom. I'll help you," Vince said. "He'll pass out right off."

"He's been drinking, Vince?"

"Damn right!" Vince went behind the chair and pushed it through the hall as Jett followed. Blake's wailing was loud and furious, and the shaking did not stop. In the bedroom he took his hands from his face and the huge tears streamed down his cheeks and off his chin to his shirt. He kept saying, "Jett!" and then his words lapsed into incoherent tones punctuated with moaning sobs. Vince stripped him to his shorts.

"Pull the cover off the bed," he ordered Jett.

She was crying too. Her hands shook as she turned the blanket down and backed up to let Vince lift Blake and plop him on the bed. He pulled the covers back up over Blake's shivering body, and he started to go from the room. Jett looked back at Blake nervously, but called out to Vince and caught him there in the hallway.

"You didn't get to Richmond?"

"Your father didn't want to go to Richmond, Jett."

"But he had to see the doctor."

"No, he didn't. I should have known better. Listen, Jett, he's a hopeless case. You've got to believe that. He'll rot if he keeps thinking he's going to get better. The doctor told me, Jett, there's nothing that can be done for him. Nothing!"

"Vince, he was drinking! You let him drink! He—"

"I didn't— Oh, God!" Vince brushed her aside. He thought of telling her then, of telling her what he had told Luke, but he could not.

The tears poured from her eyes and she said, "My poor Bunny," and Vince knew it would do no good to tell her. Their world was lopsided, upside down, inside out. Vince did not know how to straighten it out. He just wanted to get out of it.

"He'll sleep until morning, don't worry. Let *him* tell you about it, Jett."

"I'll get him a wet rag for his head," she said. When Vince left, the cold water was running in the kitchen. She was dabbing at her eyes with a handkerchief, and searching through the drawers for a cloth to put on Blake's head.

Chapter Eighteen

THE DOORBELL was ringing. Jett sat up and listened. Dust-spangled sunbeams filled her bedroom, and the breeze from the open window swayed the chintz curtains. She reached for her watch quickly and saw that the time was eight o'clock. Again the bell sounded, and Jett slid into her slippers, grabbed her robe, and hurried down the hall to the door.

"What is it?" She stared through sleepy eyes at the colored worker from the farm.

"Mr. Vince said to give this to you. He's gone, ma'am. Left an hour ago. Said good-by to everyone."

She took the envelope from his hand. "What do you mean, he's gone?"

"Done left, that's all. Picked up and took off. Said good-by and just took off, ma'am."

"All right," she said. "All right." She shut the door and walked over to the kitchen table. Her hands pulled at the envelope and ripped it open. The brief note read:

Dear Jett,

I want to say good-by to you this way. There isn't any way for me to tell you how much I've valued your friendship and the years I've known you here at Bel Aire. My fondest hopes and my sincerest wishes for your happiness will be constant. I think you had better explain to Blake that I'm leaving. The reason should be obvious to him, but if it is not, please tell him for me that I felt I could no longer do my work well and enjoy business relationships with him as I had tried to do in the past. Five years is a long time, and a man gets tired. Take care of yourself, Jett.

VINCE

She reread the letter, unable to believe what it said. Her back slumped against the chair and she held the paper in her lap, remembering last night. Vince had acted as she had never known him to act last night, curt and bitter, angry with Blake. And he had said Blake would never get well. Jett turned the thoughts over in her mind, recalling Blake's horrible scene, his hysteria, his drunken breath, and the impatient way Vince had desposited him at the house and refused to tell Jett what had happened that evening, why they had not gone to Richmond. Blake had gone to sleep immediately, just as Vince said he would, and Jett had lain awake in her bedroom trying to put the pieces together—torn between thinking about Blake and thinking about her own problem with Luke. But Blake was also her problem. He was *the* problem, and if what Vince had said was true and Blake would not walk again, then all hope was disabled too.

But Vince leaving Bel Aire! It was preposterous and incredible! If there were any explanation, it would lie with Blake now. Jett got up, measured out the coffee, and set water to boil on the stove.

His jaw was relaxed, his mouth open wide, the black hair falling forward on his forehead, the long arms limp at his sides. Jett went to the window and opened the blinds, leaving the coffee steaming on the table at the side of his bed. She took his shirt from the chair and put it over her arm.

"Blake?"

He stirred, pressed his lips together, and drew the sheet up to his head.

"Blake, wake up!" She put her hands on his shoulders and shook him gently. He still reeked of liquor and stale smoke. His eyes opened when she pulled the sheet down. "I brought some coffee," she said, "to make you feel better." She put her hands beneath his arms and pulled him to a sitting position.

Blake held his head with his hands, his bare chest chilled by the draft from the open window. She handed him his shirt and he wiggled into it.

"Hello, Cricket."

He reached for the coffee cup and put it to his lips, sipping the hot liquid carefully. Jett sat in the chair facing the bed.

"Sorry," he said, sighing. "I'm sorry, Cricket."

"It was awful, Blake. Awful!"

"I know."

"But—why? You know you aren't supposed to drink. You never could drink, and—"

"I know. I know," he said with a trace of irritation.

She waited until he had a few more sips of the coffee. He looked dissipated and old, his face haggard, his eyes bloodshot. Someone would have to tell him. *She* would have to tell him. Now.

"Blake, Vince quit!"

He looked at her amazed, the wrinkles above his eyes emphasized and enlarged as he frowned. "Quit?"

"Yes. He left me this note. Sent it up by Toby just a while ago."

"What's it say? Read it, I can't. I can't see anything."

She read every word slowly, carefully. When she was finished, she handed the paper to Blake. "What does he mean?" she said. "What happened last night, Blake?"

"So he quit, huh?" Blake wrung his hands and clenched his teeth. "Walked out. Well, I suppose it's just as well he did."

"Won't you tell me what happened?"

Blake looked at her and forced a smile. "Yes, I'll tell you, Cricket," he said. "I'll tell you exactly what happened last night. Remember, we left to go to Richmond. Remember that?"

"Yes, Blake."

He was giving himself time to think, time to get the the details of his story straight. Again he sipped from the cup of coffee, and fumbled at the side of the table for his cigarettes. "Got to have a match, baby."

"Don't smoke now, Bunny."

"Got to," he said. He found a matchbox in the pocket of the shirt he wore, tore off one, and lit it, sucking the smoke into his lungs. "Well," he continued, "it seems Vince didn't want to go all of a sudden. He stalled me. Told me we better eat first, and ordered me a drink. I didn't want to drink it, but I did. I figured the guy was doing me a favor by driving me all the way up there to Richmond, and I could be civil enough to have a drink with him. It was a double shot, Cricket, and you know how I am with liquor. Vince took his time eating and I finished ahead of him. He said I might as well have another drink and relax because we'd be driving a long time. I had another. The first one weakened me and I couldn't think straight. Vince started to argue with me about going to Richmond. He said I wouldn't get better and he said I didn't have an appointment. I did have an appointment and I knew it, but I couldn't make him believe me. The drinks were getting me dizzy and I couldn't convince him of anything."

Blake inhaled on the cigarette and watched the smoke pour out. Jett was paralyzed by his words.

"He ordered me another and another. I know I'm a fool when I get near liquor and don't know how to stop. I kept drinking, but I had an idea what he was up to. He was trying to keep me from getting to Richmond. He didn't want me to keep my appointment. I asked him— begged him to take me, and he laughed. He said it was too late anyway. You know the rest. He brought me back here. When I saw you, I just broke down, that's all. You were the only one who ever believed in me the whole way. The only one who ever believed I'd get well again."

Jett sat still, the terror of the scene vivid in her imagination.

"Another thing," Blake said slowly. "He even tried to

plant suspicions in my mind about you. About you and
Hetherington. He said you and Luke Hetherington were
seeing each other behind my back."

Her face went white.

"A bunch of lies," Blake said. "I know that now, honey.
But last night I wasn't sure. Do you understand that?
Last night, Cricket, I wanted to kill myself when I heard
him talk that way."

"But why—why would Vince ever—" Jett left the sentence unfinished. She sat looking at her hands, which
were wet with perspiration.

"I don't know why," Blake said. "I really don't know,
Cricket. Some men get jealous of what other men have.
Jealousy is a strange thing. It worms its way inside you,
and once it gets there it grows until it's bigger than you
are and you can't handle it any more. I think that's what
happened to Vince. Hate to believe it, but what else can
I believe?"

Vince. The one person she thought she could trust. Jett
was sick all over, sick and numb.

"So now things will have to be different around here,
with Vince gone. I think I'll make other changes, too—
the ones I talked with you about. Get rid of Kane and get
a new man to take his place." Blake put the cigarette out
and went on talking. "Maybe that's what we need at Bel
Aire. Changes."

Jett could not concentrate on what Blake was saying.
Her mind rushed to the thought of Blake's firing Willie,
of what Willie would tell him. She had to prevent it,
perhaps pay Willie to leave the farm.

"Jett?"

"Yes, Bunny?"

"I think the best thing is to forget all of this. I'll make
another appointment in Richmond, and get men to
replace those two."

"It must have been terrible for you," she said.

"Would have been, Cricket, if I hadn't had you to

come home to. But I have you. I'm richer for that. Nothing can take that away from me. Nothing!"

He believed that, too. He did not want to admit that he had listened to Willie Kane's lies and let them gnaw away at him as they had. Blaming everything on Vince that way was cowardly, he knew, but Blake could not reprimand himself for what he had told Jett. The important thing was to keep her love, never to let it stray that far from him again. Eventually he would replace Hetherington, too. Even if there were no truth to the story Kane had told him, he did not want to chance the possibility of its happening. While he was searching for someone to take Vince's place, he would be thinking about a man to manage Bel Aire, someone like Luke Hetherington, but older, perhaps. With a family. The farm would brighten up considerably if there were a family living there. Jett would have a woman to befriend, and Blake would enlarge the cabin, make it a more suitable home.

"Tell you what, honey," he said to her. "Swing that wheel chair over here. I'll clean up and we'll go down to the track. You can take a ride while I attend to this business, get the ads placed and notify the fellows there's an opening or two. Then after that's done, we'll take the day off. How about that? We'll just take the whole day off and have fun together!"

"I'd—love it, Blake." She recognized the sound of disappointment in her own voice and feared that Blake might have recognized it too. But he did not. He laughed and grabbed for the small trapeze he used to boost himself into the wheel chair. "Meet you in twenty minutes," he said. "We'll go down together."

At the paddocks, the swipe handed Luke the saddle, a cheap one with the skin ripped off it, the kind used to get a new animal initiated to the feeling of the weight on its back. The horse danced on her hind legs and reared off from the spot while Luke grabbed the halter shank and pulled her to. The saddle fell lopsided on the smooth black back of the beast, and the swipe pushed it up in place.

"There!" The swipe caught the sweat rolling down his face with his jacket sleeve.

"Let her walk around for a while. Don't want to try getting on her yet," Luke said. "She's a real wench!"

The horse took off, kicking and swaying her large frame to shake the saddle from her back, but it stayed. Luke walked back to the fence and watched her while the swipe leaned down to tie his shoe in the center of the runway.

"Get clear of her," Luke yelled at him. "She's mad!"

He pulled a tall weed from the field on the opposite side of the fence and bit into it, letting it droop from between his teeth as he straddled the fence bar. The swipe came back to where Luke sat and leaned on the white railing.

"Hear about Gellert going?" he said to Luke.

"Yeah, something about it this morning."

"Never think a guy steady as he was—" The swipe shrugged his shoulders without finishing the sentence. "I don't know," he said. "You never know, I guess."

If Jett did not show up on the farm before noon, Luke would go up there, and Blake Black be damned! Vince had convinced him that Blake was a madman, corrupt and rotten, swallowing Jett up in his diseased schemes, crippling her in a much more horrible way than he him-self was crippled. Luke was not surprised when he heard that Gellert had packed up and got out. He would have done the same thing if it were not for Jett. He had spent the long night lying in the bunk, hearing the tin clock tick morning in, the aura of paralysis gripping at him too because he could not go to Jett then and help her. Luke wondered if Vince had told her what he had said last night at The Blue Mill. Would she see it all then, or would it merely suffice to craze her further, make her more wary of hurting her father? It was not simple, the way Luke had thought it was. Even Jett did not know how very complex it was.

"Think we ought to try her, or let her run longer?" the swipe said.

"Let her run," Luke answered. "I'm going down to the office for a while. Let her run, and then put her out in pasture. We'll try her tomorrow."

If Blake were there, he would call Jett at the house and tell her he had to see her. Crossing over to the barn, he glanced back at the paddocks with a twinge of bad conscience. It was impossible to work with these thoughts paramount in his mind.

"Luke!"

She was standing just inside the barn, her suede coat thrown over the shoulders of her white shirt, the dark jodhpurs tight on her legs, her black boots shiny and clean. A colored bandanna covered most of her hair except for the soft waves above her forehead, and her face was drained of color, pale and drawn. Luke hurried to her, and reaching her, let himself be pulled in behind the rolling red door of the barn. It was damp and dark there, and her pressure on his hand was intense.

"Luke, where's Willie Kane?"

"Are you all right?"

"Yes! Luke, help me find him! Blake's going to fire him and I've got to get to him first. I'm going to pay him off. It's the only way, because—"

"Shut up, Jett!" Luke shouted his words and took her by the shoulders. "Listen to me now. Stop this! Your father knows about us! Willie Kane can't tell him anything he doesn't know already. He can't tell Blake anything he hasn't already told him! Do you understand, Jett? Your father knows everything! Last night he made up that story about going to Richmond! He was trying to trap us, Jett! That's why Vince quit!"

"Luke, please!" She struggled to be free from his hands

but Luke held her firmly. "Blake told me what happened last night. You'd never believe it, Luke, what Vince did! Yes, Blake does know, but it's not Willie Kane who told him. Vince told him! Don't you see, Luke? If Kane goes to Blake now, he'll think there is something to the story. He'll—"

Luke said his words fast, angrily. "I punched Kane in the nose and kicked him in the ribs that day he tried to get you at the quarry. I told him to get out of Bel Aire. He didn't go, Jett. He didn't go because Blake told him he didn't have to go. Kane squealed to Blake, and then Blake made all that stuff up about the Richmond trip to see if Kane was telling him straight. Now listen to me." He forced her to hear him despite her attempts to get away from him. "Last night I walked into the restaurant where Vince and Blake were sitting—waiting until Blake decided it was time to go back to the house and catch us. When Blake saw me he decided the story was wrong. He was sorry then. Vince *told* me this, Jett! You've got to wake up, honey! You've got to!"

"You've got it all wrong, Luke!"

He released her and she stepped back, rubbing her forehead.

"Jett, did you ever think of this? If your father really loved you, wouldn't he ask you how you felt about me if he suspected anything? Wouldn't he be glad you were happy if you announced that you did love me? What kind of abnormal human being is he, Jett? God, honey, don't you see? Don't you know what your father is trying to do to you?"

She pulled the coat around her shoulders and stood silently. The dank smell of the barn filled her nostrils; the thoughts churned through her mind, never focusing, never stopping their circles and zigzag turns. What Luke had said about Blake's being abnormal was spotlighted in her brain. She wanted to turn the light off because she saw herself standing under it too, along with Blake.

"Luke, I don't know how to say this. I've thought of it before. Mostly before I met you. Blake and I had a fight about it once."

"About what?"

"About him—and me. About the way we felt about each other. Blake knew it wasn't right. He wanted me to go to college because of one night when—well, he kissed me and it wasn't right. I didn't want to go, Luke. I didn't care whether it was right or not. . . . Do you see what I'm saying?"

He stared at her, trying to assimilate what she was telling him.

"Whether you see it or not, don't blame everything on Blake. You see, we never have been like other people. We've been different, Luke, separate. Bel Aire has been like another planet, a little world where we lived. He was all I ever knew. All I ever loved in my life. I was always with him. Even when I began to grow up and know I wasn't like other daughters and he wasn't like other fathers, it didn't make me stop feeling that way about him. Luke, you were the one that made me stop feeling that way. You— Luke, say something to me. I've never told anyone this before. I feel—"

He put his arms around her and let his lips touch her forehead. It was something alien that he did not understand. He understood the significance of what she had told him, but he had to think back on everything, on the way he had first loved her, on her attempts to be rid of him, her fear of Blake—everything. More and more he hated Blake Black, for if Jett knew no other world but Bel Aire, Blake did, and the blame was his.

"It's going to take you a long time to know the truth about your father, Jett. I don't care how you felt. You were a child!"

"I felt that way four months before I met you, Luke. I didn't grow up in four months. Don't put all of the blame on Blake. Don't put any of it on him."

"I'll get you out of here, Jett. We'll get married. Now."
She stepped back from him. "You haven't understood
anything I've said. I love you, Luke, but don't you see
I can't just suddenly believe my father is a bad person?
Not just like that--not ever. I've lived with him all my
life—known him, loved him. What you've told me about
last night—the Richmond trip, all of it— Luke, I'm sorry.
I don't believe you. It isn't that I think you're lying.
Maybe neither of us knows the truth. Maybe that's it.
But the truth isn't your version! Blake wouldn't lie to
me. I know that."

"I can't say anything to you, Jett. You're deaf to everything! Deaf and blind!" Luke turned from her and
walked to the door. He stood looking out at the paddocks
and pastures, at the swipe leading the horse around the
ring. "The only thing for me to do is to get out, like Vince
did. I won't do that yet because I can't. I'll be around
for a while yet, and maybe some of it will sink into your
mind. Maybe you'll know that what I'm telling you is
God's truth."

Jett stood alone inside the barn. From the other end,
the door rolled back and a swipe led a horse in, kicking
the stall open and steering him in. Jett pushed the straw
under her feet and pulled her coat around her shoulders
again. She walked out of there slowly, breathing in the
fall air, crisp and fresh. Then she began to hurry, her
coat flapping behind her as she ran across the walk,
through the field on the other side to the mess and the
garage behind the mess.

The truck was backed out in the driveway, the smell
of gasoline lingering, the gravel spotted with oil stains.
Jett looked around her but did not see any sign of him.
A swipe was asleep near the front wheels of the truck,
his head resting on the bumper. There was no one in
the garage. She was afraid that she was too late, that
Blake had reached Willie Kane first. If she had not spent
that time with Luke, she might have prevented it.

She poked the swipe with her hand. He opened one eye, and then, seeing her, the other, jumping to his feet.

"Ah was jest cat-napping fer a—"

"Never mind that," she said. "Where's Willie Kane?"

"Him? He ain't got no haul t'day. Don't know where he's at. Could be at the mess, maybe, ma'am. I'll hunt him out if you like."

"Tell him I have a haul for him."

"I don't know if I kin find him fer you, ma'am, but I'll sure try and tell him that if I see him over there."

The boy scratched himself vigorously and began walking off toward the mess. Jett looked on all sides of her, but saw no one. She stood there, undecided, looking back into the garage again.

"He ain't back in there." From the front seat of the truck she saw Willie raise himself, his yellow teeth grinning at her, his head looking up at her from the side of his neck. "That boy knew damn well where I was! Got these jigs scared blue of me! Lots of folks round here scared of me now."

"I want to ask you something. I'll pay you for an answer."

He opened the door and fell out, dragging his stubby legs along as he came over to her. "You're scared too, ain't yuh?"

"I'll give you ten dollars just to say yes or no. Ten dollars!"

"Go ahead and ask me. Go on. I'll tell yuh."

"Tell me the truth. Will you tell me the truth? I won't do anything to you, or tell anybody anything about this, if you'll just answer me."

"Go ahead, go ahead, missy! What yuh wanna know? Didn't know I had any sense a person could ast me a question to answer."

Jett looked at him hard. "Did you tell my father what you said you would at the quarry? *Did* you?"

Willie slapped his hand on the baggy knee of the

trousers and giggled. "Naw! Scared, wasn't yuh? Still scared!" He giggled again. "Gimme the ten dollars."

"I'll give you more," Jett said, "a lot more, if you'll go away."

"No!" Willie sneered at her and walked away from her toward the entrance to the garage. "No!"

Jett followed him. "Listen to me. I'll make it worth your while! I'll give you fifty dollars to clear out of here. I've got fifty in cash, do you understand?"

"Your boy friend kicked me. It ain't nice to kick an old man."

Willie walked into the garage and took a cloth from a hook at the side of the wooden wall. He wiped his hands on the cloth and ignored Jett. She stood at the entrance. "How much will you take to leave this place? Look, you're going to be fired anyway! Do you hear me? I know you're going to be fired because my father told me that this morning. If you get out now, I'll pay you. Get out and don't come back."

"You got the fifty dollars with yuh?"

"Yes, in cash."

"You try to trick me."

"I'll show you," she said. She unbuttoned the top pocket in her jodhpurs and took the green money out. "Here!" She walked over to him, holding the money in her hand.

"Put it on the shelf up there," he said.

"How do I know you'll go?"

Willie's shoulders shook and he laughed. "How do you know?" he said. He turned around and looked at her. "I'll go! Don't you worry, I'll go."

Jett put the money on the shelf. "If you don't go . . ." she said, but she did not finish. Willie kicked her in the ankles hard, pushing her over backward at the same time, and she hit the dirt ground of the garage with a thud, the wind knocked from her. He leaped on her and slammed his palm over her mouth, his eyes glistening with fever. "Sure I told yer daddy, missy. Told 'im everything I seen! 'Member what I seen? 'Member all the things I seen when yuh didn't know I was watching? Oh, I was watching, all right!"

She kicked at him, jerking her body to one side, her mouth sliding from his hand long enough for her to scream out, and then he caught her again, this time stuffing his fist in against her teeth. She forced her jaw down on his flesh, but with his other hand he hit her stomach hard. Again she screamed, but the sound was muted by his arm striking out across her mouth as he leaned forward.

"I'll knock yuh out! I'll knock yuh out if yuh scream, 'cept I want to see your eyes."

His weight was insufferable and Jett could not breathe. For a moment she gave in, her muscles loosening, her head falling back on the dirt while Willie Kane reached a hand inside her blouse, tearing her straps.

Then, in one rush of strength that she forced through every part of her body, she half raised herself, screamed shrilly, and scratched the sides of his face with her hands so deeply that Willie fell back and she was able to bring her boot to his chin. He stumbled as he got up, stumbled again as he moved forward in an attempt to reach the shelf and the money, but he saw the colored boy then, standing near the entrance, his eyes brown circles of shock, and Willie Kane began to run, down the driveway, fast, past the boy, too fast to be caught. The boy took off after him anyway.

Jett lay still and then slowly sat up, her head throbbing with pain, her ears barely able to hear when Luke reached her. He had heard her scream from the walk and come running. Seeing Kane and the colored boy running down the drive, he had known where she was, and his feet shot toward the garage. Some other men were running too, behind him, but he had reached her first and gone to her, bent over and tried to raise her to her feet.

She cried out from pain, from the harrowing experience, from having Luke touch her again, a cry filled with fear and hurt and thankfulness for Luke's being there.

The two men reached the entrance to the garage just as Luke got her to her feet.

"Kane!" he shouted at them. "Get Willie Kane!"

One was a swipe, the same swipe Luke had worked with, and he grabbed the other's coat. "I saw him! Come on!"

"Jett! Oh, my God, Jett!"

She clung to him, crying, hardly able to speak. "You were right, Luke. You were right!"

The men were gone. Luke took Jett over to the side, leaning her up against the wall while he bent and picked up her coat, putting it around her, his arm supporting her waist. She began to cry louder, her voice high, hysterical.

When Blake heard the screams he was in front of the office, and they came from the garage, which was on his left. He pushed the wheels of his chair frantically, running it across the lawn, his arms straining. He could see only the back of the garage, and he was several yards from there when Kane ran down the gravel drive. Blake saw nothing. The wheels skidded on the grass and he pushed at them, his forehead dotted with sweat, his stomach heaving with fear. At the side of the garage he could hear her screaming, and he caught hold of the rake leaning against the front before he worked the chair around the corner. He saw Jett then just as he reached the entrance, the rake on his lap, his hands forcing the chair over the final bump to the dirt ground of the garage.

Luke Hetherington's back was to him, and he saw Hetherington's hands at her waist. Her face was scarlet, the sound of her voice choking out, tears streaming from her eyes. Blake's hand left the chair and he grabbed the rake. He heard Jett scream, "No!" and suddenly, with the rake raised, he lifted his body, pulled himself up, his feet touching the earth, swinging the rake at the back of Luke's head, before Luke turned and ducked. The rake crashed to the earth as Blake took two steps forward and sank down at their feet.

The dirt filled his mouth and he could not turn. He could not save Jett, he thought, he could not! Hetherington's voice barked out words he could not hear, but he could hear Jett's voice. He did hear what Jett said.

"Luke, help me with him!" She was still crying. "Darling, darling, help me with Blake!"

He swallowed the dirt and wished he were dead.

Chapter Nineteen

THE BEDROOM was dark, the house still. Blake wondered if it was day or night, and what day it was. He stretched his jaw, feeling the pull of the gauze bandage, and shut his eyes to think. Slowly he began to remember some of what had happened. He remembered Doc Sellers.

"You're a lucky man, Blake Black," Sellers had said. "I don't know how in the name of the good Lord you took those steps, how you even got up on your two feet, but you did. You did, and you will again. I didn't believe it myself, but Kingsley confirmed it. Do you hear what I'm saying to you? You're going to walk again!"

He remembered the strong smell of the salve they had spread on his legs, the way they had pulled at his feet, the feeling there, the voices mumbling around him, Sellers and Kingsley talking low while they bent over him.

The dreams too; he remembered them. Jett! He could remember her only in the dreams, running to her, never catching her, running and calling after her, standing at the top of the stairs, and then falling, swirling through black space, unable to see her at the bottom. Jett!

He tried to count the hours he had been there in that room. Forty-eight, maybe seventy-two. Had Jett been with him? Blake rubbed his eyes and tried to make the days come clearer. His mind was drugged, his body limp, exhausted. In a moment, he knew, he would fall back into sleep again, but now he had to force himself to try to remember more.

"Darling, darling, help me with Blake."

Yes, he remembered *that*.

He was not sure that he had not imagined her screams from the garage. Why had she screamed? He had wanted to crack Luke Hetherington's skull open with the rake because he had thought Hetherington was hurting her.

"Darling, darling . . ."

Then he had walked. A miracle had made him stand and walk. He had walked to save Jett from harm, and he had fallen in the dirt, and down there, with his mouth full of it, his head rubbing in it, he had realized that he was wrong. He had been wrong a long time, a lifetime.

Blake leaned on his elbows and raised himself in the bed. He listened but heard no sound in the house. He called out, meekly at first, and then louder. "Jett! Jett!"

She was not smiling. She came through the door of the bedroom almost automatically, her face showing no emotion, her dark eyes level, meeting his.

"Jett, I was afraid you'd be gone."

"No," she said. "No. I've been here." She stood at the side of his bed, a streak of light from the open door shining on her plaid skirt, her hands at her sides, her fingers clenched into her palms.

"I'm going to walk again, Jett."

"I know."

"Jett, I don't know what to say. I lied to you. I want to tell you that."

Jett said, "I know that, Blake." She looked down at the floor. "I found that out from Willie Kane. I guess we both lied to each other."

"You mean—about Hetherington."

"Yes," she answered, "about Luke."

"I thought he was hurting you, Jett. I heard you screaming and— Why were you screaming?"

Jett sat down in the chair by the bed. She told him what had happened without looking at him. He lay back listening to her, her voice steady, her words flat, telling him everything.

She finished by saying, "I love Luke, Blake. I love him and I want to be with him—always."

"Jett?"

"What?"

"Look at me."

Her eyes stared at him, her lips tight together.

"You can get to a point where saying you're sorry doesn't mean anything at all, but you have to say it anyway because it's how you feel. I must have been sick a long time before I ever crippled myself, Jett. Somehow you just grew up and I never thought about much except the way you grew, the fine person I knew you were—having you with me. Other folks didn't matter much, and I guess I never gave you a chance to let them matter to you, either. I loved you and I wanted to do everything for you, but I tried too hard, some ways, and I didn't try hard enough others. Jett, what I'm trying to say is all muddled up in my mind, but I'm glad about you and Luke. That'll tell you something."

"It hasn't all been your fault. I don't know whose fault it was. We made a mess of things, Blake."

She wanted to reach out and take his hand, but she could not. The warmth was cemented inside her. She felt that she would never be spontaneous with him again, never be close to him.

His eyes shut as he turned his head away from her. "I want to tell Hetherington I'm—sorry," he said.

"He's in the living room now."

"You think he'd come in for a minute?"

"I'll see," Jett said. She knew how cold she was, how much she was hurting Blake, but she could not be different. She walked out of the room and down the hallway. The rain was falling lightly outside, and the square window at the front of the living room was wet, the afternoon sky outside gray. Luke sat in the big chair, his back to her, the smoke from his cigarette curling up in the air and drifting away.

"He wants to see you," Jett said.

Luke dropped the magazine he was reading and stood up. He took Jett's hand in his. "Was it rough?"

"Pretty bad. It was me, mostly. I can't seem to look at him."

"Does he know everything?"

"Yes," she said. "I told him."

"I'll go on in," Luke said. "Try to rest, honey, please! Just sit down."

After Luke left the room, Jett stood by the window, watching the rain fall on the grass outside, run along the rocks near the hill, and trickle down the paths slowly, winding in and out of the brush there. If it had not been for Luke these past three days, Jett knew she would have broken down, collapsed under the weight of her thoughts, her anxieties. She had meant what she said to Blake. It was not all his fault. There had been lies on both sides, tricks, deceit, and fear. She did not reject him because of his part in it, but because now that it was over, now that every stone was unturned and the crawling life that had existed there was exposed, Blake seemed foreign to her, a man she no longer knew. Jett walked over to the couch and sat down. She slipped the loafers from her feet and stretched out. The rain on the roof had always sounded beautiful and peaceful in the past when she had lain listening to it, but that afternoon it had a morose tone. When Luke came back into the living room, he found her there, asleep.

Raol was waiting in front of the school, the yellow slicker too large for him, the matching yellow hat pulled down over his eyes. Luke honked the horn, and Raol came running to the truck.

"You're late. We been out ten minutes."

"I'm sorry," Luke said. "I was helping Jett."

"Her father still sick?"

"He's getting better, Raol. He sat up this afternoon and talked to everyone."

"Do you like him, Dad?"

Luke turned the car off the highway on the back road

leading to Bel Aire. "Like him? Yes, I think I do, Raol."
He reached in the glove compartment for his cigarettes
and pushed the lighter plug in, waiting for it to pop out
hot. He remembered what Blake had told him, and he
thought to himself how easily he had condemned Blake
in the past, how ready he had been to hate him. Yet that
same kind of snap judgment, that bullheaded unwillingness to find out all the facets of a situation, to mull them
over and let them sink in, was the very way trouble
began. Luke wondered if he would have had the courage
Blake had shown that afternoon—the courage to weep in
front of a man who had been his enemy, the courage
to ask for forgiveness.

"We're going up to the Blacks' for dinner," Luke said,
"but don't roughhouse too much. Mr. Black will be
sleeping."

"After dinner, can I go with Jiffy till eight-thirty?"

"O.K., but that means an extra hour's sleep in the
morning. Want to be fresh for school every afternoon."

"Jiffy says school is for the birds," Raol grunted.

When the dinner was over, Raol put his rain boots
back on and went out the kitchen door, only pausing long
enough to wink at Jett and salute Luke. Jett and Luke
sat across from each other at the table, Jett sullen, her
hand holding the empty coffee cup as she looked toward
the tray on the drainboard.

"He didn't eat much."

"Did you talk with him again at all, Jett?"

She looked at Luke and shook her head. "I wanted to,
but I couldn't."

"He's going to need strength to walk. In fact, he's going
to need strength to keep on living, Jett. I know how
you feel, honey. I hated him, at first. Hated him. But
listen to me, Jett. It's always easier to excuse your own
mistakes. It's never easy to excuse someone else's. That
takes character, honey."

"It's all dead inside me. Everything I ever knew with him. Everything we did together. Dead!"

Luke walked over to where she was sitting. He leaned down and kissed her, and her arms came around his neck. "Jett, it can be all right now. It can be, Jett, if you can just make yourself understand your father. Listen, you understood him as a man for a long time. Try to understand him as a father as well. He was different. Sure, he was different. But Jett, he made those mistakes because he did love you. Maybe a hell of a lot more than most men love their children, and sure, maybe too much. Kids always find it easy to blame their folks for what happens to them, even when they know they were in it up to their necks too. They still blame the father, or blame the mother. Someday Raol will be blaming me, Jett, and maybe it'll hit me like a thunderbolt that he was right. That I raised him wrong from the first holler out of him until the time he was old enough to stand before me and call me names. But, honey, after that's all over, the child's got to grow up. You've got to grow up, Jett. You've got to see that your dad is human too. He's not a god, and he wasn't—wasn't ever anything but a man. There's no Santa Claus, either. Do you see what I mean? Blake proved a lot of things to me this afternoon. I don't get over things easy. But I forgive him, and I learned plenty from him."

"Maybe we could—both go in and talk to him now. He's awake. I told him I'd come back later."

Luke carried two dishes over to the sink and heated the coffeepot on the stove. "You go in alone," he said. "I'll be out here. But you go in alone. Just talk with him for a few minutes. That'd be important to him. Try it."

There was a light coming from the crack under the door of the bedroom. Jett stopped when her hand touched the brass knob. God make me do it! she said to herself. Make me do it!

She turned the knob slowly and pushed the door open.

Blake was sitting up in bed, the pillows supporting his head. Words did not come to her, no words came as she stood in the doorway, and then she took two steps across the room.

"Hi," he said. He looked away from her, and in that instant she wondered if she would be able to walk closer to him. She felt frozen. Blake reached out for the package of cigarettes on the bed table. His hand shook, and he could not seem to pick up the package. He grabbed for it again and the water glass fell to the floor, the splinters of glass scattering along the wood at the edge of the rug. The sound startled Jett. She came awake, and looking back at Blake, she saw his face color, his lips pull together.

Then she did move, quickly, easily. She walked to the side of his bed, picked the package of cigarettes up, and stuffed it into the pocket of her blouse. Her eyes met his squarely.

"You smoke too much," she said. "You smoke too damn much, Bunny. You know that, don't you?"

The smile came automatically to her lips; a surge of relief overcame her and grew up inside of her. Blake grinned, and simultaneously their easy laughter filled the room.

Chapter Twenty

A WARM May wind swept over the terrace, carrying the aroma of honeysuckle and ripe apples. Up at the end, near the trellis with the green vines, Dr. Sellers stood beside Luke. This was the first time he could remember seeing Hetherington without the round skullcap, the torn work pants, and the baggy shirt. If he had not seen it with his own eyes right there, Doc would not have believed that Luke owned a fine suit of clothes like those blue ones, with a crease in the pants too, a fresh tie, and a crisp white shirt.

Jett smiled as she came toward them. Her dress was a light pink color, her black hair held two matching pink rosebuds at the side, and her dark eyes shone when she looked at Luke.

Doc held his breath. He watched Blake sitting over in the iron porch chair, and Doc shut his eyes and prayed hard. He waited, oblivious of the words spoken, his eyes on Blake as he sat perfectly still, his head held high, staring up at them. It made Doc nervous, but he had to keep watching him, keep saying his prayer over and over.

Finally, the time came.

"Who gives this woman to be married?"

Blake moved forward in the chair. He stood, the canes supporting him. Inch by inch he stepped on the slate under his feet, slowly, carefully, his face solemn but proud. When he reached Jett's side he stopped. Doc could feel his heart pounding inside him as he took his place alongside Blake.

"I, Luke, take thee, Jett, to be my wedded wife, to have and to hold from this day forward, for richer, for poorer, for better, for worse, in sickness and in health, to love and to cherish . . ."

The minister's voice was precise and low, and Luke's
words were clear, meaningful. Young Raol stood on the
other side of Blake, his small face serious, his hands behind his back, the white trouser legs straight, the cuffs
lapping over onto his spanking-clean white shoes. Jett's
voice came then, soft, slow, her head turned toward Luke,
her hand holding his tightly.

"I pronounce you man and wife."

They held one another, and Doc looked away when
their lips came together. Then suddenly the voices all began at once. Raol's squealing high and laughing, the
minister's droning out professional congratulations,
Luke's answer, and Jett's voice as she turned to speak to
her father.

"Bunny! I'm so happy!" She hugged him and for a
moment Doc couldn't believe his eyes. The canes were on
the slate floor, and Blake was standing unassisted, his
arms holding his daughter, his face creased with smiles.

Doc, Raol, and Blake stood in the doorway late that
afternoon. Jett handed Luke the bags and he piled them
in the back seat of the car, and when it was finished, she
walked over to the three of them. She shook Doc's hand
and kissed Raol on the cheek. Stopping in front of Blake,
she looked at him a moment before she put her arms
around his neck.

"Bunny, you shouldn't be on your feet for such a long
stretch."

"I'll have two solid months to rest, Cricket."

Luke walked up to them and grinned. "You're going
to need that rest. When we get back, this old farm's really
going to jump."

He lifted Raol high in the air. "You keep after the
carpenters, son. Don't let them put closets where we want
bedrooms down in the cabin."

"I won't," Raol promised. "I'll be bossing them."

Luke put his hand out to Blake. "Don't let the boy get

too big for his britches," he said, "and make him study that alphabet!"

The car went down the hill slowly. Blake sighed and sat down on the porch steps. Doc took a clean handkerchief from his pocket, mopped his brow, and blew his nose vigorously.

"You know what Jiffy says?" Raol said. "Jiffy says you're my grandpaw, Mr. Black."

Blake looked at the boy and nudged the Doc. "By golly," he laughed, "by golly, Jiffy's right!"

He looked back at the road. The car was out of sight, the dust on the dried mud road settling. A hot sun bore down, promising a warm day. It was the beginning of a new summer.

THE END